GEMS FROM MY PEN

A collection of Short Stories

JB. Woods

ISBN 13: 978-1481002608
ISBN 10: 1481002600

Dedicated to my wife *Jenny* for her continued support and encouragement...

Contents

The Author has chosen to advise on some of these stories although they contain no gratuitous violence, bad language or sex but they could possibly offend as there is innuendo.

He also admits to using some pictures off the Internet in the Public Domain to give an added highlight to the stories and not for financial gain.

𝕮illa and Cyprus Airways Flight - CY 283

𝕮illa - Genus: Larus Argentatus Scousus.

𝕬 herring gull to you and me, hatched into a one parent family in Liverpool on the roof of The Lord Nelson Hotel in May 2003. Her father had died under the wheels of a Number 21 bus whilst dining on a Big Mac.

Hungry males who had a fancy for day old chicks had eaten her brothers, Ringo and John. From then on Mom only scavenged at night to give Cilla a better chance of survival.

The choice of nesting site was no coincidence. The location had been passed down, beak to beak over generations. Situated behind the Liverpool Empire and Lime Street Station and a short distance from London Road and the infamous Lime Street it was a scavenger's delight.

Fed on a diet of chips, beef burgers and kebab, and on Saturday nights, when a better class of people came out of the Theatre—Cod in batter, it was little wonder that Cilla was classified as clinically obese at six weeks old.

Mom knew it was going to be hard work getting Cilla into trim for a gap year trip South to the sun, but she persisted with the flapping exercises and at eight weeks Cilla managed a short haul flight over to the Station roof. Her landing skills were below standard and she chipped a piece out of her beak when she nose-dived onto the glass canopy.

The next day they extended their flight to St Georges Hall and on the third day she was quite out of breath when Mom took her to the Pierhead. However, she soon learned to glide and pick out the air currents and on the second week they skimmed over the Mersey to New Brighton where she was introduced to KFC chicken wings. She instantly disliked gurkins. After having eaten one she had lost control over her ground-speed for a couple of hours, going forward in spurts of jet propulsion. Disconcerting, especially when landing.

After her initial three weeks training and a kilogram lighter, Mom declared Cilla ready for her adventure.

'You're a big Gull now, Cilla, and it's time too see the world. We'll see you in a couple of years. Remember, avoid trouble with those large silver human birds, don't fly too high, and watch out for marauding cocks who want nothing but sex.'

'But, Mom, I'm brown and ugly.'

'Not for long, dearest. You will soon change into a beautiful adult. Don't forget now. A fuelling stop at New Brighton, then follow the estuary and turn left at Anglesey where you will meet your cousins. Got your passport. Good, off you go.'

There followed a minute of beak bashing and sobs before, with a squawk, Cilla took off into the blue yonder. Mom followed her to the Pierhead and shed a tear as her offspring disappeared into the early morning mist.

—

Cilla felt a little peckish at Llandudno and ignoring Mom's advice glided down to find a snack. The local Mafia took offence at this interloper and harassed her until she moved on. Tired and hungry she stayed overnight on the Great Orme before heading for Anglesey. Arriving too late to go with the organized flight to the Sun she had her fill of leftovers from the Irish ferries.

The following day she set off South. She by-passed Haverford West. Lundy Island was hopeless as the greedy seals had left nothing. However, the buffet in Newquay was first class.

She turned left again at Lands End towards the Isle of Wight and caviar in Cowes before hitching a lift on a ferry across the Bay of Biscay to Santander.

Carefully working her way around the coast she eventually reached Gibraltar four weeks after leaving home. Mom had said, go to the Canary Isles, but Cilla met an old crone on her last sea legs her web feet shredded like sun dried tomatoes, who said to her, 'Go into the Med, dearie. Much more fun.'

So it was, Cilla turned left yet again and into the Mediterranean. She dawdled up the Costa's, past Benidorm and onto Marseille before wintering in Majorca where she had her first moult.

Now brilliant white and silver grey with black wingtips and a ginger tuft on her head she set off for Corsica, Sardinia and Sicily, but she found these islands disappointing as there were no lazy tourists discarding leftovers.

Still hungry, she hastily took off for North Africa where the Arab fishermen were more to her liking. They threw scraps and undersize fish to her and as the African coast was off the gull touring map she had little competition.

By November she reached Egypt where food in the Nile delta was plentiful and she settled for a week in Alexandria. Here she met a male cousin from Wales.

Now a full sixty centimetres in height and a wingspan of one-hundred and twenty she was heaven to him. He landed alongside her and said, 'Say, chick, what say we bash beaks on the lighthouse tonight?'

'I'm not a Gull like that, Tom Jones. I'm saving myself until I get home and I'm leaving tonight.'

'Go the anti-clockwise route, babe, and visit Cyprus. Paphos is a good watering hole and Bar Street at dawn is 'A la Carte.'

'Thank you. I think I will.'

Her mind made up, she had a good meal down at the fish dock where they were gutting the days catch, before resting until nightfall. At sunset she took off for the long night flight to Cyprus.

The next morning at eight-forty-five an exhausted Cilla spotted the broad expanse of Paphos Airport and in her weariness she forgot her Mom's warnings about aeroplanes.

'A little rest here before breakfast, I think.'

Approaching across wind she glided down. Left turn into the wind. Webbed under carriage forward as air brakes, a little reverse thrust. Too late she saw a shadow looming over her.

With a 'Whoosh!' and a terrified 'Squawk!' she was sucked into the gaping mouth of the Rolls Royce

Turbo fan engine. Decapitated, plucked, sliced and grilled in three seconds. Cyprus Airways Flight CY 283 had landed.

—

Bing! Bong! 'Attention! Passengers for Flight CY 283 Larnaca, Paphos to Heathrow are warned there will be a short delay owing to a Technical fault.'

Poor Cilla, after that brief encounter with an Airbus A320 she had been demoted to a Technical fault and that is how I will remember her. It took four hours and three telephone calls to Rolls Royce before we could set off for the UK on a blustery November, Monday morning.

***

ꓑaith, ꓘope & Charity

The icy blast of a late Autumn wind made him shiver and ruffled the golden coat of Faith the retriever who sat patiently by his side. She turned her head and looked at him imploringly with her big brown eyes and gave a little muffled bark. She longed to gallop over the moorland stretched out before them above the town but she felt the sadness and the emptiness in his heart.

———

For nine months they had met here on the fallen tree trunk while their dogs romped around doing things that dog's like to do. It had been five days a week at first and then three as the treatment took its toll. Her long wavy blonde hair had disappeared to be replaced by a woollen bob cap and her clothes became baggy as she lost weight but her effervescence and cheerfulness never left her as she always remained optimistic about the future.

In the final weeks it had dwindled to two visits as it became harder for her to climb the hill to the moor. They sat longer, holding hands, wrapped in each others thoughts as the visits became less frequent.

8

When he had suggested that he meet her lower down the hill to make it easier she had refused saying it was not fair to the dogs and she likened the experience to being on top of a world that was pulling her inexorably down.

Then there was nothing. Just a lonely emptiness. For two weeks he had come everyday in hope that she may be there but he knew in his heart that the end had come. That she had thrown off the shackles of life and gone to a peaceful place free of the pain she had endured without complaining.

He had cried quietly to himself those first few days of loneliness up there on the hill. Only Faith had felt his grief and sat with her head resting on his knee trying to comfort him.

She was also depressed at the loss of her playtime friend, bringing to an end the empathy she had with her canine companion.

He unfastened her lead, 'Off you go, gal, have a run.'

She also had lost the will and sat patiently beside him. Taking another quick peek at him she saw the far away look in his eye and knew that they would be here for some time. With a long doggy sigh she lowered herself to the ground and lay with her head resting on her front legs and began dreaming of four foot of retriever hormones who had been her consuming passion for all those months.

A wintery gust blew dried up leaves past her nose but there was something else in the wind. Her nose twitched. She sat up and sniffed. There was no mistaking those pheromones. She barked, pushed her head between his hands and nudged his lowered head.

'What is it girl? You ready for home? I suppose your right.'

She barked again furiously dancing up and down and ran along the path a short way towards the scent that was coming her way. Then she heard it. An answering bark. He heard it also and sat upright listening, wanting in all the world to see her coming over the brow.

'Go on, girl! Go and meet them.'

No second bidding was needed and away she went just like old times, disappearing along the path to welcome here soul mate.

He stood up unsure what to do, shuffling his feet and self consciously patting his hair into place, wishing and hoping at the same time. He could hear the dogs barking and yelping, getting closer.

'That's a lot of barking for two dogs.'

Over the hill came not two dogs, but three, running like free spirits. They leapt and frolicked and took off down the slope in a frenetic Olympian challenge.

He stood entranced as she came over the hill and along the path with her golden tresses blowing freely in the wind. His mind asked the question. 'Wait a minute, is it her, or her reincarnation wearing the same deep pile sheepskin coat?'

A quick pinch assured him he was not dreaming. 'It can't be.'

As she came closer she smiled in that unmistakable way. Time was running backwards— 'This isn't possible,' he muttered.

She stopped a few paces from him and spoke and he felt dizzy and faint. He covered his face and rubbed his eyes hardly daring to look at the vision before him and then sat down sharply on the log.

She spoke softly. 'It's the right dog, so you must be, David?'

The voice, it was her. He looked up still unsure of himself. 'Yes,' he replied lamely.

'I'm Jackie's twin sister.'

He stood up hurriedly. 'Oh… I do apologise. How uncivilised of me. How do you do? I was taken aback and just a little frightened. Disbelieving in fact. I have been so wrapped up in myself. I thought I was dreaming.'

He brushed his hands down his coat and shook hands with her.

'I'm Jenny,' she said, 'We are, I'm sorry, we

were, identical twins. She talked of you and your dog incessantly. She loved you. Did you know that?'

'I loved her. I even asked her to marry me but she would have none of it, nor would she tell me her proper name. She said that she was not going to burden me with her misfortune and I must look for someone else and not grieve too long when she was gone. She was incredible. Please sit down. It's quite a comfortable log.'

'Thanks, I will. It's rather a steep climb up here.'

She sat next to him, close enough for him to feel the warmth of her and he was startled to find she even smelt the same.

'Your dog,' she spoke with the same merry lilt in her voice. 'Faith, isn't it?'

'Yes,' he replied. 'I knew her dog was called, Hope, and in the absence of her proper name that's what I called Jackie. What do you call your dog?'

'You've guessed, it's Charity, and I see they get on famously.'

He turned to look at her amazed at how alike she was to her sister. She smiled at him and her eyes were smiling also.

'It's getting late now, Jenny. Can I walk with you back down the path?'

'Yes, please do.'

He whistled. Faith pricked up her ears and in an

instant she was running towards him with the others close behind.

'Do you look after, Hope, now, Jenny?'

'Yes. He and Charity came from the same litter. Jackie and I lived in the same house so they've never been apart.'

'Err... I... I don't know how to say this. May I walk you home? Jackie wouldn't let me and I would very much like to see where she lived.'

'Please do. Will you continue coming to the moor to walk, Faith?'

'Yes. How about you?'

'I think I'll be coming a lot more. The dogs love it here don't they. It would be a shame to break up the threesome.'

He glanced over his shoulder for a nostalgic look at the log which had been their meeting place and then up to the sky and mouthed a quiet—'Thank you'—for this second chance at happiness.

The laughter in her voice as she called, 'Come on,' told him there was Charity in life after all.

***

A LONG SHOT

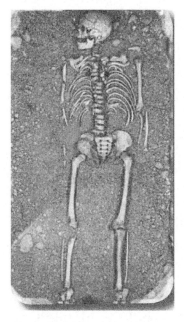

Detective Inspector Will Scarlett trod warily down the marked path through the crime scene. He stopped by the side of Detective Sergeant Littlejohn and surveyed the upper body of a skeleton poking through the mulch in a thicket surrounding an enormous oak tree.

'What have we got here, Sergeant?'

'At first glance, sir,' said Littlejohn, 'it would appear we have a murder victim who has been buried, in my humble estimation, for at least two years, probably longer, which would account for the deteriation of the body.'

'How did you determine that from this pile of grubby dog bones, Sherlock?'

Used to the putdowns of his senior Littlejohn ignored the remark and with his pen torch explained his theory.

'Between the left second and third ribs, sir, we have serrations which can be attributed to a sharp weapon of some sort. A stabbing, maybe?'

'Any identifying material or artefacts.'

'No, sir. The teeth are in poor condition which leads me to believe that we are dealing with a tramp or vagrant and they would be of little benefit for I.D. purposes.'

'You can't tell his age then?'

'No sir. If it was a horse it would be easy, but us humans, once we have our final set stay the same throughout our life. We just lose 'em.'

'How's that then?'

'Horses teeth progressively protrude forward as they get older, sir, so by the angle of the slant you can guestimate their age.'

'Alright, Herriot, have we any witnesses.'

'No sir, it's a bit late for that, but the blonde lady over there with the dog discovered it.'

'That's what I meant, idiot.'

'That's not what you said, sir. You meant, who found it?'

'I suppose I'd better speak to her. What's her name?'

'It's Mrs Marion Loxley, sir. She lives locally.'

Scarlett surveyed the medium built woman whose blonde hair was covered by a flowing diaphanous head scarf and observed mentally. 'She would be a fine draw for any beau.'

'Sgt, while I speak to Mrs Loxley arrange for a tent and lights over the body and tell forensics when they get here I want something yesterday.'

He turned away and walked over to her.

Scarlett raised his hat a millimetre. 'Mrs Loxley, I'm Detective Inspector Scarlett of the Nottingham Police. Can you tell me the circumstances that led to your discovery?'

She smiled disarmingly. 'Why yes, Inspector. I was walking my dog, it's the first chance since yesterday's storm, and I let him off the lead when we entered the wood. He's an enthusiastic animal and he tears around as if he's never been free before, but this time, when we got here, he barked and disappeared into that thicket. I shouted Dicky, but he continued barking and yelping and I could hear him digging so I rushed over to see what the fuss was about,' she pointed towards the body, 'and that's what I found. I called 999 immediately on my mobile.'

Scarlett rubbed his forehead with the back of his hand. 'Dicky, ma'am?'

'Yes. It's short for his pedigree name—Richard-John-Plantagenet of Fenchurch.'

'Tricky that.' He nodded in the direction of the skeleton. 'And Dicky did all that, you didn't touch it?'

She screwed up her face. 'Err, no Inspector, it's icky.'

'Thanks, ma'am, you can go now, we'll be in touch.'

'There's one thing you should know, Inspector. I feel I know him.'

'How do you know it's a him?'

'It's just a feeling. You know—de ja-vu.'

———

Later that day Scarlett and Littlejohn went to the Forensics Lab, donned paper overalls and overshoes and pushed their way through the plastic screen doors into the sterile interior of the laboratory where the rotund, balding, Dr. Francis Tuck, greeted them cordially.

'Mornin' Inspector…Sergeant. I hope you're ready for this.'

'I've seen it all before,' said Scarlett, 'what've we got?'

Tuck led them over to a dissecting table upon which was the unearthed skeleton and they stood around it. He picked up a scalpel and used it as a pointer. 'Firstly, we have a male murder victim.'

Littlejohn swelled up with pride and smirked at Scarlett, who scowled at his sergeant's prowess.

'See here,' continued Tuck, 'there are scratch marks on these upper ribs indicating a sharp weapon of sorts. That's what killed him eventually, he probably bled to death. Secondly, this body is old, some of the bones are calcifying but the peaty ground around the tree has preserved him pretty well.'

'Any idea who he is and how old?'

'I was coming to that.' Tuck picked up the right hand of the skeleton. 'We're still waiting for the carbon dating results but I think your man is quite ancient. Meanwhile,' he lifted the fingers one at a time, 'there are signs of Arthritis in the first and second fingers and wrist. Excuse me, Sergeant.'

He pushed past Littlejohn and went to the other side of the table and picked up the left hand. 'And this hand shows signs of Arthritis across the palm, like the fist was clenched. This way, gentlemen.'

He led the way to a side table where a number of artefacts were laid out and picked up a slender quill.

'This was under the skull and on examination it's the tail feather of a pheasant. Probably used as an adornment.'

He held up some discoloured fibres. 'These were found under the body and after closer examination are the remnants of a green material, probably a jacket, and this!' He held up, with a note of triumph in his voice, a small arrow head. 'This,' he said again to emphasize his point, 'is the murder weapon!'

Before anyone could reply an eager lab technician

burst through the screen door.

'Mr Tuck, sir,' he called excitedly, 'It's amazin'!'

'What is, Dale?'

'Carbon dating, sir. It says those bones are 800 years old.'

'Are you sure?'

'Positive, sir, we double checked.'

Tuck spun round and faced the baffled Scarlett and Littlejohn triumphantly. 'There you have it, gentlemen. Your final proof. You've dug up—ROBIN HOOD!'

***

The slings and arrows of outrageous -
'𝕾𝖊𝖈𝖗𝖊𝖙𝖘.'

 The sounds of Chris de Burgh extolling the virtues of his scarlet woman faded in the frosty December air and 'Sherwood Close' became alive with other noises. Car doors banged, high pitched voices shouted half meant well-being's and stiletto heels shivered unsteadily towards copycat redbrick boxes.

The Christmas party at John and Rosemary Little's house was a success as always and their inner circle of friends had begun to depart in various stages of inebriated excitement.

Robin Bowman sought out his wife Elaine, but instead he spotted the ultra-feminine blonde vision of Rosemary making a bee line towards him.

'A lovely evening Rose.'

He lowered his head to give her the customary 'goodbye' hug and kiss and much to his surprise she threw an arm around his neck, thrust her hips tight into him and kissed him full on the mouth.

'I love you,' she said breathlessly in his ear.

He lifted his head and nervously glanced across the room towards the tall figure of John and was relieved to see him preoccupied with other departing guests.

Not quite knowing what to say, he untwined her arm and said quietly, but firmly. 'Rose, I love you, dearly, but this is not the time. I will see you on Wednesday as usual.'

He saw the beginnings of a tear glistening in the corner of her eye and he gave her a squeeze and kissed her on the forehead. 'When the time is right, love, I will tell Elaine, but you must be patient.'

'You're right,' she whispered, 'but hurry, I ache for you,' and wistfully she added, 'take care until Wednesday.'

She turned away and with a half-hearted smile waved to someone about to leave.

His wife, Elaine, provocatively attired in clinging green sequins, came up behind him and linked an arm through his. Her lips were moist and her eyes sparkled with Champagne fuelled anticipation.

'Hi, handsome, are you set, because I am. Let's go before the mood wears off.'

They said their goodbyes, but there was no sign of Rosemary, and John made her excuses as he waved them off from the front door.

'It doesn't matter, John,' Robin assured him, 'it was a great night, give Rose our love.'

He smiled quietly to himself as they dashed, giggling, across the road to their house and he wondered what delights Elaine would serve up that night as she was a woman of great enterprise.

John also smiled secretively as he watched the lissom figure of Elaine and he turned to seek out Rosemary to burn up the passion that stirred within him, unable to wait for Wednesday's passionate excesses at the 'Foresters Hotel'.

——

The landlord of the 'Foresters', Bill Tuck, a portly man whose hair was receding quicker than the tide, gave Robin a knowing wink as he served him a beer and a glass of wine. Nothing was said, but he had been witness to these Wednesday goings on for six months and had sometimes rostered Elaine and John into the same room just for devilment while at the same time avoiding several close calls in the olde worlde lounge while the sheets were changed.

Robin joined Rose in the alcove by the fire and she snuggled up close. His hand dropped to her thigh and she wriggled sensually as the last tingles of spent passion quivered through her body.

She moaned quietly and whispered, 'Robin, I don't think I can take this much longer. I love you and it is driving me mad waiting for Wednesday to arrive.'

He desperately sought the right words and he said, in what he hoped was a sincere voice, 'I promise you, Rose, I will tell her, it won't be long now.'

He deliberately looked at his watch. 'Look at the time, I must ring Elaine and let her know I'll be late.'

Flipping open his cell phone he speed dialled Elaine at the same time he smiled and blew a kiss at Rose.

He listened for a couple of rings before he became aware of the opening bars of 'Greensleeves', the familiar dial tone of Elaine's phone. Pin pricks of anxiety coursed through him, adrenalin fuelled messages pinged in his brain.

'Keep calm,' he said to himself. 'go slowly towards the sound.'

He stood up and looked over the settle dividing their alcove from the one next door and saw Elaine's green leather handbag lying in the corner unattended. Breathing a sigh of relief he switched off his phone and turned to Rose.

'Let's go for a drive, Rose. It's a lovely afternoon, a quiet walk by the river will be just right to end the day.'

His hopes of a quick retreat were dashed when a husky voice, which he knew intimately, said, 'Fancy seeing you here.'

He swung around, and leaning with his arm outstretched across the settle he smiled weakly at Elaine who stood before him flushed in expectation of the primeval gymnastics to come.

'I just dropped in for a couple of beers, dear. In fact I was trying to call you.'

His attempt at shielding Rose failed dismally when she stood up and said, 'Who is it, Robin?'

She gasped and the colour drained from her face when she saw Elaine. 'Oh, oh, dear,' she stammered.

'Oh dear,' said Elaine, mimicking Rose and taking delight at watching her squirm with embarrassment. 'Oh dear, indeed.'

The wavy haired figure of John came down the stairs in the lobby, walked across to them and wrapping his arms tight around Elaine he said in mock disapproval, 'Oops, who have we here?'

Robin shook his head disbelievingly and Rose opened her mouth to speak when Elaine said, 'Now seems like a good time to tell you, Robin. I'm leaving you. I'm going to live with John.'

There was silence for a moment, when Robin, in a moment of distracted, patronizing arrogance, hooked his thumb towards Rose.

'No problem,' he sneered.

The repressed anger of super cool Rose, exploded. Her metal adorned handbag came up in a swift, swinging arc and hit Robin behind the ear so hard that he took an involuntary step forward.

'So, I'm now considered—No Problem,' she said, 'you self-serving chauvinistic bastard!' John and Elaine stood wide eyed and incredulous. Who was this seething tigress. 'If you imagine for one moment I am moving in just for your convenience, you, you, marital pimp, you have another think coming. I can't believe I fell for that old line.'

Roses shoulders drooped and she pointed at John, dejected, but resolute. 'You're going to regret this. Get a good lawyer. And you Elaine, enjoy little things, do you,' A reference to a part of John's anatomy, 'that shit doesn't know what loyalty is. You're welcome to him.'

She scrambled out of the alcove with as much decorum as she could muster and pushed her way out to the car park with her tears of grief at the indignity of it all flowing freely.

Elaine looked steadfastly at Robin, reached out and ran a green lacquered fingernail down his cheek and said facetiously, 'You never could keep a secret, could you, never mind a woman. Sell the house, you can keep the dog. Oh, and Merry Christmas!'

She turned and walked towards the stairs, John shrugged and followed.

Robin waited until the coast was clear,

straightened his tie, smoothed his hair and sauntered through to the bar. He walked over to a dark skinned, sensuous woman with long black hair who was sat provocatively on a stool and put his arm around her waist and kissed her on the back of the neck.

'Hello, Marion.'

'You're late, Robin.'

'I had some strings to cut. Oh, by the way, do you like animals?'

She put a hand around the back of his neck, kissed him hard, and purred, 'I especially like animals.' She scooped a room key from the bar and slid with feline grace off the stool. 'Come on, I'm feeling hot.'

Robin smiled as he picked up her coat, winked at Bill Tuck and said, 'Happy New Year!'

***

The Roman Samaritan

Through the dust thrown up by the many tramping feet on the baked mud road emerged a detachment of Roman infantry of the elite Lanceari[1] of the Xth, 'Fretensis' Legion. Camp followers and store wagons covered in thin white powdery sand straggled along behind like an army of ghosts.

Their progress was watched by a shepherd with an injured animal slung across his shoulders herding his sheep and goats. What thoughts he had of these invaders of his country were hidden behind the immobile mask of a face burnt black by the sun.

At the head of the column rode Paulus Tiberius, recently promoted to Primus Pilus[2] for his daring leadership at the siege and desecration of Jerusalem. His was the task of carrying the news of the victory to Rome, by none other than Titus, son of Emperor

Vespasian. It was 70AD, the time of the Jewish, Diaspora.[3]

The column came over a rise and the soldiers breathed a collective sigh of relief to see their onward journey was downhill. The white band of the road snaked away into the distance to the port of Ceaserea which was hidden by the blue grey heat haze. The plain of Samaria below them, where all the major conflicts of the Holy land had been fought, shimmered in the glare of the sun.

As they approached a brown stone village Paulus raised his hand to halt the column by an olive grove that would offer shade for his soldiers.

He called forward another mounted soldier. 'Centurion, disperse the men amongst the trees. We will stop here tonight. Have the women go to the village well and restock the water.'

He called for his servant. 'Sergio!'

Close by a voice with a hint of whimsy, answered. 'Yes, Master?'

Why did he bother? Whenever they stopped his servant appeared as if by magic.

Paulus reached up to remove his helmet and his fingers tingled when they came into contact with the hot metal. He eased it off, to reveal a ruggedly handsome man with close cropped black hair, dark brown eyes, and an aquiline nose. A scar ran diagonally from the centre of his forehead across his right eye, down his cheek and continued down to his shoulder and arm, a memoir of a close encounter with a Frankish warrior in an earlier campaign. It gave him an aggressive appearance contrary to his personality.

'Sergio, some water before I have you flogged.'

He took the proffered goatskin and a cloth to wipe away the sweat that ran down the side of his head tracing two rivers in the dust that caked him in a beige mask. He tilted his head and took a deep swallow from the skin.

When he lowered it something caught his eye. A movement in a rocky outcrop at the top of a nearby hillock, a mere flash, or was it his imagination?

Curiosity got the better of him. 'Sergio, prepare a meal. I am going to the top of that rise to look around.'

'You go alone, sire?'

'Yes.'

'Take care, there may be Sicari.' Sergio spat out the name given to the marauding Jewish zealots.

'I heed your warning, but I have no fear of the dagger men. I will take the goatskin. My throat is like a desert.'

He pulled his horse's head around, gave her a dig in the ribs and set off at a gentle cantor through the white narcissus that grew at the side of the road and into the swathes of anemones which covered the hillside in a blood red mantle.

An excellent horseman he guided her with precision around rocks and boulders until he was some fifty metres from the summit.

Dismounting, he threw the reigns over her head and stood quietly for a minute or so, watching, and listening. He decided that he must have imagined whatever it was that caught his eye, but taking heed of his servant's warning, he took a second sword from his saddle roll and slung it over his shoulder the hilt sticking up between his shoulders. With his regulation sword and short stabbing sword hanging from his belt he felt quite secure.

'It's about time someone invented something lighter than these things,' he grumbled to himself.

He took a long draught from the goatskin and hung it from the saddle before stealthily climbing the short distance to the summit. He rounded a huge parched rock and put a hand out to steady himself, quickly withdrawing it with a curse. The heat of the sun had made it white hot.

'What a god-forsaken country this is. It's only late spring and already it burns like a baker's oven.'

He crashed to his knees on some loose shingle, thankful for the protection of his metal shin guards. Muttering, he turned over to a sitting position and surveyed the scenery around him.

To his right, through the haze, he could barely make out the town of Samaria some five miles distant. To his left, in the direction from which they had come, the road and the town of Shechem where the column had stayed the previous night were lost amongst the mountains and valleys of inner Palestine.

'Help!'

Paulus grabbed for his sword. The cry had been so quiet and rasping he was not sure he had heard it. Was it the wind playing tricks?

'Help! Help me.'

There it was again, louder this time. There was no mistaking it, someone had used their last strength to hail him.

Paulus scrambled up with his sword at the ready and made his way cautiously around the rock, apprehensive as to what he would find. Stealth was impossible. His feet scrabbled for a grip on the loose shards. His foot slipped and he threw out his left hand to steady himself.

Instinct made him withdraw his hand immediately as he felt the scales of a blunt nosed viper coiling to strike. He slashed down with his sword and watched in amazement at the thrashing headless body.

Paulus became aware of the same rasping, pleading voice.

'Water, please.'

Throwing caution to the wind, he sheathed his sword so that he could use both hands to pull himself the last few yards around the rock. What confronted him in a small hollow under the boulder was not a brigand, but a boy of about fifteen in obvious distress. Burnt red, his lips bleached and cracked and the once white toga stained by the dust of the roads, defiance shone through the brightest of blue eyes.

Paulus jumped down into the hiding place. The lad cowered away held up an arm to ward off this fearsome looking Roman.

Raising his right hand, palm outwards, Paulus spoke to the lad in Greek, the common language of the Mediterranean. 'Have no fear, I mean you no harm. Wait while I fetch water from my horse.'

He turned away and scrambled out of the hollow to return a few minutes later with the goatskin. 'Here, drink your fill, slowly now.'

The boy grabbed the goatskin and drank deeply, gulping the water down.

Paulus snatched the skin. 'I said, slowly, do you want to die of the cramps?' He gave it back. 'Now steady.'

He waited for the boy to drink his fill. 'Now tell me who you are, and how you got into such a mess?'

Now that the dust of Palestine had been cleared

from his throat the youth said hesitantly. 'My name is, Iasonos, sire. I am a refugee from Jerusalem where I was a servant who escaped to Pella with my master and the Gentiles before the siege. I took a chance to flee from my bondage and ran for the coast to search for a boat to Cyprus.'

'Why Cyprus,' Paulus queried.

'It is my homeland, sire. I long to look once more upon Mount Olympus,' and feeling a little daring in the face of his inquisitor, 'What do you yearn for?'

Paulus hesitated, nonplussed, 'Err, the red roses my mother nurtures in the garden of our villa outside Rome.' He screwed his face up and shook his head and once more asserted his authority. 'Enough of this, are you a Gentile?'

The boy drew back, afraid of the vengeance carried out by the Roman army against their enemies.

'Easy,' Paulus spoke gently trying to allay the lad's fear, 'I have no quarrel with the Gentiles. I have some belief in your God and his Kingdom in Heaven, although I am not wholly convinced. Answer the question.'

'Yes, sire. I am a Gentile.' Feeling braver he continued, 'You would be right to believe, he is a true God, not an idol. The Master showed us the way.'

'How would you know that? He died thirty seven years ago.'

'It is in his teachings, sire,' replied Iasonos, 'handed down by his Apostles. My father heard the preaching of Paul, who was Saul. That is when he converted to Christianity.'

'Paul, aye. Now there was a troublesome man. Hush, I hear someone coming. They look for me. From now on you use your Roman name of Jason and no mention of Christianity. Stay there, I will speak with them and have you cared for.'

Paulus climbed out of the hiding place and went to meet the search party led by his servant.

'Sergio!' Paulus called out when they were still a short distance away.

'Yes, sire.'

'Return to the camp and fetch two of the women. Beyond that rock is an injured boy. Tend him and bring him down. He has water, but will need sustenance. He is badly burned by the sun. Cut some Aloe to sooth his sores. Hurry!'

The search party turned about and Paulus followed them electing to walk instead of riding.

———

Several hours later Paulus called for his servant. 'Sergio, how fares the lad?'

'He is responding well to the ministrations of the women who have adopted him, sire. He walks very weakly, but a good nights rest should restore him. His burns will take a little longer.'

'Good, bring him here.'

Five minutes later Jason was brought to him and he noticed that he was of medium height with a good physique.

'Jason?'

'Yes, sire.'

'You will accompany us, but you will have to work when you are able.' He turned to his servant. 'Sergio, he will be your assistant and my sword carrier. Give him three sesterce a day and find him some better rags to wear. Now leave me in peace.'

A little over a week later when the boat entered Paphos harbour, Paulus called Jason to him and spoke to him in a low voice. 'Yonder is your home, lad. I will not take it amiss if I am minus a servant on our departure. Take one of my swords for your protection and here is a letter with my seal should anyone stop you. You will be safer here than Rome this day.'

'I don't know what to say, sire.'

'Say nothing. Your endless twittering drives me to distraction. Be gone, and take great care.'

'Thank you, sire, and may you seek the way of the Lord. You have the compassion of a true believer and looked upon me as did the Samaritan in his teachings. I will always look upon you as a friend and not a Master.'

Paulus gave him a gentle cuff around the ear.
'Go!'

***

[1]Lanceari – Light Infantry or Lancers
[2]Primus Pilus – Senior Centurion
[3] Diaspora – Dispersion of Jews

***

A Christmas Carol Conundrum

*An adult '**Henrietta**' story suitable for children.*

December 23rd.

The Hen Choral Society were assembled in the henhouse to discuss the possibilities of extending their range after last year's success at the Farmyard Christmas party.

'What are we going to sing this year, Henrietta?'

'Cluck, cluck,' said Henrietta deep in thought as she walked backwards and forwards down the centre aisle

'What about, 'We three Kings,' said Harriet, Henrietta's sister.

'We can't do that silly, there are seven of us,' said Henrietta with a toss of her head.

'Why don't we do, 'While shepherds watched their flock,' chirped Helen from the back.

Henrietta stopped and looked at Helen quizzically.

'Shepherds are in short supply nowadays,' she said with a shake of her head, and she continued walking.

Hermione raised a wing and said shyly, 'Err, Henrietta, I thought maybe we could do 'Silent Night.'

Henrietta paused in mid stride, head cocked to one side, like chickens do, and thought for a moment. 'Good one that, Hermione, but considering the racket we get from fireworks, mobile phones and the like, I don't think it's appropriate anymore.'

There was lots of clucking and cackling as they talked amongst themselves and Henrietta continued her walking deep in thought when blonde Felicity cooed huskily from her box.

'I think 'Good King Wenceslas,' may be alright with the snow around this year.'

Henrietta stopped in mid stride, spun around and stalked back to Felicity, who, seeing red in Henrietta's eye, cringed to the back of her box.

Henrietta studied her pitifully for a moment before saying. 'You do try, don't you. Felicity, and don't flutter your eyes at me. That carol is all about a King looking out from his overheated castle and watching one of his serfs gathering wood and woe betide that serf if he picks up a dead pheasant and takes it home. He is thrown into the castle dungeons and forgotten.'

'Oh, you're so smart, Henrietta.'

Silence returned and it was not long before the snuffles and sighs of tired chickens wafted around the closed confines of the Hen Union house, when quietly, oh so quietly a little voice said,

'The Holly and the Ivy, anyone?'

'Who said that,' said Henrietta crossly, upset because she had been dozing off.

'Err, err, I did,' said Heather timidly.

Henrietta replied with quiet exasperation, 'Heather, dearest, they have dragged out most of the hedges today or cut them down with those mechanical choppers, which means no two Holly bushes can get together long enough to create the berries. It's really not practical today,'

A collective sigh went around the hut and all became quiet once more, when, from the end box, Sylvie, a German immigrant squawked, 'Vot about Tannenbaum?'

The henhouse erupted in unison, 'Oooh, shut up!'

———

Christmas Eve came and Henrietta pulled herself up to her full Rhode Island height and addressed the assembly.

'Fellow chickens and Big Red.' His arthritis was playing up and he had chosen to stay indoors. 'As we have no carol to sing I have decided that we will sit on the wall and watch the humans at their Christmas party anyway. It was such good fun last year, apart from Felicity's ordeal. Are you joining us tonight Felicity?'

'I certainly am. I wouldn't miss it for the world.'

'It's frosty tonight,' Henrietta said, 'so if Felix the feral feline is around we will hear him crunching in the snow.'

The duty chicken counted them out into the brisk night air; seven plus Red and in single file they ran through the shallow frozen snow to the corner of the barn.

Felicity, who always tried to make a good impression, ran too enthusiastically and with feet scrambling for grip she collided with Sylvie and the group collapsed into squawking domino mayhem.

After many precious seconds clucking and dusting themselves down they stood around Felicity in a half circle.

With wings furled on hips Henrietta looked down at the hapless bird and shook her head in dismay. 'Essex girls,' she muttered, and turned away.

She poked her head around the corner of the barn, gave the all clear and sprinted over to the garden wall, closely followed by the others, and with a short flap of their stubby wings they hopped onto the wall and carefully made their way to the spot opposite the Farmhouse living room window where the Browns had conveniently left the curtains open. They fluffed up their feathers and settled down to watch the fun. Big Red stood at the end wondering what the fuss was about.

Fixated Felix the frozen feral feline eyed them, but thought better of it after last year's debacle and sat quietly watching from a distance.

Freddie Fox padding up the lane in the shadows with sentient* sensitivity, sniffed supper.

He stopped and nosed the air searching for the scent and in the moonlight he saw the Hen Club enthralled by the party fun inside the house. Surreptitiously, sneaking silently, with slinking synchronicity and sniffing softly, he sidled secretively towards Sylvie.

Big Red heard Freddie crunch the snow and with surreal, savage, swiftness, swooped swiftly, extended sensors searching with super sensitivity for the soft skin on Freddie's nose.

Henrietta and the girls screeching simultaneously with steely saltation* joined Red and pecked, punched and pinched perspicuously* until Freddie scarpered, scrabbling in salcadic* shock for shelter.

Mrs Brown the farmer's wife burst out of the farmhouse door with a shotgun in her hands and shouted, 'Hey! What's going on? Who's there, I've got a gun.'

At that moment, the off key melodies of a Christmas Carol wafted up the lane. It was Farmer Brown coming home after a merry night at the 'Red Lion' pub singing at the top of his voice.

'That's it,' shouted Henrietta with surprise, 'Why didn't I think of it before? Come on girls, back on the wall, and you Red.'

In the spotlight from the open window the Choral Society lined up with Big Red as baritone accompaniment and Henrietta chanted, 'In time with Farmer Brown, one, two, three…

'Oh come all ye faithful,
Joyful and triumphant,
Oh, come ye, Oh come ye, to Be-eth-lehem...'

Hearing the musical commotion the children ran outside into the farmyard and young Johnny Brown shouted, 'Henrietta, you've done it again, this tops even last year.'

Sylvie rubbed her head against Big Red's chest and whispered huskily, 'Ober hünchen*, v'ere is dis— Bethlehem?'

*Ober hünchen: Chief Hen.

*Salcadic: Twitchy.

*Sentient: Sense or Perception

*Saltation: Leaping or dancing.

*Perspicuously: Clearly expressed, easily understood.

The complete collection of **'Henrietta – Tales from the Farmyard'** suitable for children of all ages can be found on Kindle or Amazon Books

***

Devotion
or
'Is anybody there?'

Harry wandered into the kitchen with slow, deliberate movements done with much thought, because, as a consequence of his actions his fingers were tingling and he had pins and needles in his legs.

He put his whisky glass down on the kitchen table and looked around once more before he reached into the cupboard where they kept the medicine basket and to his satisfaction he found another packet of Maisie's painkillers.

Ignoring the warning label he took two tablets and swallowed them with a mouthful of whisky.

'How long do these things take,' he muttered.

Going over to the sink he dried the breakfast things and before he put them away remembered fondly how he used to tell her off for leaving knives and forks sharp end uppermost in the cutlery holder.

He stepped back and looked around once more, trying to remember how she liked it. A shiver ran down his spine as the emptiness of the bungalow echoed around him and a feeling of devastating loneliness swept over him. With a sigh he wiped down the work-surfaces and spread the cloth over the taps to dry as she always told him to do. He hung the damp tea towel over its rail and slid it out of sight before picking up his glass and swallowing two more tablets.

'I'd thought two strips would have done it,' he murmured to himself.

Back in the living room, he straightened cushions and filed away the old newspapers before going to the hall cupboard to fetch the Hoover. It took only a few minutes to manoeuvre around the furniture cursing as a stubborn piece of fluff refused to be picked up and he had to bend down to remove it. He wobbled a little as his head spun with the effort and he was beginning to feel drowsy as the tablets began to take effect.

Putting the cleaner away and using his handkerchief as a duster he slowly edged his way around the room wiping picture frames and shelves as he went.

He smiled as he imagined her scolding him. 'She would have played merry hell if she had seen that,' he said speaking aloud, which only served to magnify his solitude.

He stepped back holding on to an armchair for support and studied his handy work before he looked upward and spoke as if he was addressing someone.

'We can have visitors now, love. It's all spick and span and ready for anybody,' wondering at the same time who that anyone was going to be. It appeared to be a useless exercise, but she had always said to him, 'I don't want anyone talking about us when we're gone.'

He felt tired and nauseous as he went through to the bathroom but logic told him that if he spaced the tablets out a little he wouldn't be sick. That would be pointless. He looked at himself in the mirror and watched his weary time worn, 85-year-old reflection through lonely saddened eyes as he took two more tablets with water this time.

He reached down for the J-cloth kept behind the toilet and cleaned the bath and sink and for some unknown reason he cleaned his teeth. What was left of them anyway? He only had ten and the others were false. She would have liked that touch.

'Can't have your breath smelling, Harry, she would say.'

He could see the laughter in her eyes as he straightened the towels over the rail and checked that the tassel on the spare toilet roll cover hung down at its correct angle.

Finished, he turned around and grabbed the doorjamb as he staggered. Pulling himself together, he dragged himself into the lounge and laughed when he noticed that he had subconsciously timed the video for her favourite soap as he done this past twelve months when her illness had moved into its final painful stage.

'I don't think you need that, love. Never mind, it'll give them something to talk about.'

He felt like sleeping, but there was a couple more things to do. Standing unsteadily he picked up the phone and dialled 999 and then left the handset off the hook.

Next, with arms outstretched, he worked his way down the hall and put the front door on the latch before going into the master bedroom where Maisie was lying in peace. Relief had come quietly during the night and mercifully released her from her pain.

He lay down beside her and kissed her cheek. 'I'll be with you shortly, my love, and don't be cross. It's what I want.'

—

Fifteen minutes later there was sharp banging of the front door knocker and urgent ringing of the bell. Pushing open the door a policeman entered and moved cautiously down the hall calling, 'Hallo! Is anybody there?'

***

A 'Woman in Black'

A play on Titles and quotations

'Depressed. Me? Never, but it was the anniversary of her passing and I felt like shit.'

It was mid-afternoon and too early but I felt like a drink and quite frankly **'I didn't give a damn.'**

After a **Brief Encounter** with a 'BIG ISSUE' salesman I pushed open the doors of the first bar I came to. A quick glance affirmed it was **'Rick's Bar'** but I tried my best to remain positive. I was the only patron and as I clambered onto a stool the bartender dragged himself from the TV. His name tag informed me he was Sam.

'Original,' I thought.

'Set 'em up, Sam, just you and me. Fancy a cigarette?'

He declined and poured two whisky's. I lit a Marlborough, exhaled, leaned on the bar and stared into my drink while listening to the **Sound of Music** drifting around the bar. It was Aretha Franklin singing **'The First time I saw your face.'** It stopped and Sam went to change the CD.

I said, **'Play it once more, Sam. For old times sake. Play it for me.'**

He nodded and gestured towards the entrance. I looked across and rubbed my eyes in disbelief. **'Of all the gin joints in town she had to walk into this one.'**

Wearing a black PVC trench coat fastened with a knotted belt she stood silhouetted by the August sunlight her blonde hair shimmering in its rays. She pushed her sun-glasses onto her head in her trademark fashion and sauntered towards me. I was held **Spellbound** as the coat moved sensually with her body.

She placed one immaculately shod foot on a chair and I was immediately reminded of **Cabaret.** Untying her belt she let the coat fall open. She was naked but for the sheer delight of hold-up stockings and the mingling odour of **Ghost.** I was mesmerised and my hormones went berserk. Now I knew the **Devil is a Woman.**

She slid across to me, there was no other word for it, drew her monogram in the condensation on the bar before she lifted the cigarette from my fingers, took a drag and ground the butt into the carpet. Her bright blue eyes laughed into mine as she exhaled into my face.

'Let's go, Hunter.'

'Where to?' I said, and knowing she thought matching initials were a lucky omen and we'd dallied there before, I added, 'The Dorchester?'

'No,' she replied, '**The Apartment. I feel Wicked** today.'

Uncharacteristically I threw ten-pounds on the bar and said, 'Keep the change.'

She looped my tie around her finger and I followed her stiffly to the door.

—

The bright sunlight dazzled me and I had a sudden attack of **Vertigo.** In the distance an alarm bell was clanging. 'What **Psycho** set that off,' I mumbled.

It stopped and someone was shaking my shoulder. 'Come on Hunter, you lazy, Bee. It's **High Noon.**'

I eased open weary eyes and found Jacquie my partner leaning over me her long hair caressing my chest. I looped an arm around her neck, pulled her down and rolled on top of her. Pushing myself up on my hands I looked into her beautiful face surrounded by a lake of raven hair on red silk sheets.

I knew this was **No way to treat a Lady,** but following my **Basic Instinct** I devoured her while fantasizing about my '**Affair to Remember.**'

***

BANG! YOU'RE DEAD!

'**W**here's your homework, Gordon Brown?'

'Aven't got none, miss.'

What do you mean; you haven't got none? You haven't got any.'

'That's right, miss, I didn't do any.'

'Why not?'

'Honest, miss, I tried, but I couldn't think of nothin.'

'You're in trouble, Brown. Go to Miss Beattie and tell her I said to give you five with the belt.'

'Aah, miss, that's not fair, I did me best.'

'You mean; you did your best.'

'Yes, miss.'

'Don't be cheeky, that's another five.'

'Aah, miss.'

'Are you still here?'

'Yes miss.'

'Why.'

'Cos?'

'Because, what?'

'You haven't said to go yet, miss.'

'Brown, you had better leave before you get into more trouble.'

'Yes miss, can ah go now?'

'Can you go now, what?'

'Can ah go now, miss?'

'Can you go now, Miss Watts?'

'Can you go now, Miss Watts?'

'BROWN!

He turned on his heel and fled.

—

Miss Beattie, the terror of all miscreants glowered at him over the top of her desk. 'Yes, Brown?'

'Miss Watts sent me, miss.'

'And?'

'She said to give me five, miss.'

'Give you five, what?'

'Dunno, miss, she just said five.'

'Brown, you have just earned five more for lying.'

Gordon groaned as his plan to diminish his full punishment failed. 'Ah miss, that's not fair.'

'Life's not fair, Brown.'

She lifted the heavy lid of her desk and withdrew the regulation tawse – two foot long, an inch and a half wide and the striking end cut into strips.

Gordon knew his fate having been on the receiving end many times and he stolidly held his left arm out, palm uppermost.

'The other hand, Brown.'

He groaned again, his left handed ruse had failed. Now he would be able to use his natural hand while the other throbbed as a reminder of his indiscretions.

Swish, SLAP! Swish, SLAP! Miss Beattie smiled as she laid into her hapless victim. Her breathing became faster, her pupils larger and her sensory nerves tingled with every stroke. Her torment would begin later as her sexual release would be unfulfilled.

But this time, Gordon, determined not to show his suffering smiled as she drew breath for the final fling.

Thrown into paroxysms of sensual outrage by his apparent fondness for her torture, her body tensed, her stomach muscles knotted and a wave of passion zinged through sensitised nerves ends. She moaned through clenched teeth as the belt struck its target for the tenth and final time only this time her climax was complete.

Breathing heavily she pointed to the door. 'Get out of my sight, Brown, before I give you a double dose.'

This was the first time he had witnessed the hidden, breathless siren that was Miss Beattie and he needed no second bidding, but deep down inside his

developing body there stirred a new sensation which
he enjoyed.

———

Miss Watts stood aloof and smiled smugly down at
Gordon.

'Well, Brown, are you ready to apologise for your
misdemeanours?'

Flushed by his new experience, with *wilful
expectation* Gordon pointed two fingers towards her,
cocked his thumb, and said, 'Bang, you're dead!'

***

Cupboard Love

Someone new had arrived. There had been a rumour for some time and it was Christmas when things always changed.

She tried to pay no attention to the newcomer but everyone who passed by the glass doors stopped to look in and talk amongst themselves before moving on.

The front door bell rang, and after much stamping of feet and rubbing of hands to get the winter cold out of frozen limbs, another couple were ushered into the room.

'Oh, dear, more people staring at us,' she said quietly to herself.

Sure enough, they were guided towards the doors and they peered through, spoke to each other in quiet tones before nodding their approval to the lady of the house and moving on into the dining room.

She recognised them from previous visits, but this

time they were alone.

'Thank goodness they left those terrible children behind. They make such a mess of the doors with their sticky fingers. Oh, oh, someone's coming back.'

This time they pressed closer and pointed. Her curiosity got the better of her and she half turned provocatively, her hips thrust forward. She twisted from the waist and looked over her shoulder in an off hand manner.

She gasped, 'Oh, how could they?'

Standing beneath the spotlight was a tall elegant creature with her hair piled high on her head, which made her look even taller. Her décolletage so low a heaving bosom was near to overflowing and a bow was tied beneath it accentuating the perfect symmetry of her breasts. The long fronds hung down to the floor contrasting with the swirling material of her dress, which was the palest of blues. It matched perfectly the posy of violets in her hand.

'She is not only a hussy, but she has the effrontery to wear a dress similar to mine. She steals the light also.'

Her own dress was a sleeveless, pale blue almost grey silk with a polo neckline, which clung to her sylph like figure right down to her blue sandals. Her long hair piled up into a French pleat emphasised her pale porcelain features, which gave her a

Hepburnesque quality. She threw her head back slightly and gave the new woman a withering look.

'Oh, where has he got to? He would know what to do.' She had not seen him for such a long time and she worried that he may not be there at all.

She was startled, and then pleased when the doors suddenly opened. 'What have they done to you?'

He put his hand around her waist. She loved the way he did that. His long fingers, so gentle and tender, caressed her through the gossamer silk and she tingled with delight. He moved her to one side and reached past her to move the intruder from the spotlight.

Picking her up gently once more he placed her just right of centre stage to let the light shine on her delicate face and figure, enhancing the perfect symmetry of her body.

'There you are my love. It may be Christmas but no one pushes you out.'

He let his fingers slide down her and she shivered with the thrill of his touch as he turned her slightly.

'Not too much. I don't want to look at her all the time.'

He stood back, head cocked to one side. Pleased with the outcome, he nodded his head in approval, closed the glass doors, and returned to the dining room.

She smiled with satisfaction and lowered her

eyelids to give the interloper a knowing look that conveyed the message - I am number one in this display cabinet and his heart.

***

Domestic Operating Intelligent Tool

or

DO IT!

The gentle humming from his pillow and a little nudge in the back from the body moulded sleeping surface, stirred Jim from his slumber.

'Good morning, master.'

He stretched and yawned. 'Err, what time is it, Do It?'

'It is seven o'clock, master.'

'It's Saturday, Do It.'

'Yes, master, I am programmed to call you early. You have to clean the commuter pods before you go to the Zoo.'

'Who's going to the Zoo.'

'You are, master, at ten o'clock with your son.'

Jim rolled over and looked at his slumbering wife, Donna.

'Do It!'

'Yes, master.'

With a nod of his head towards Donna, 'What time is she getting up,'

'Nine o' clock, master. The mistress has a hair appointment and shopping with your daughter.'

'Oh, I see. She gets shopping and I get the Zoo.'

'Yes, master, you are a male. Your breakfast is ready.'

'Do It, I want a full English this morning and two cups of black coffee.'

'I am sorry, master, I detect your cholesterol is high and your blood pressure is rising. You have wholemeal toast and honey and one cup of decaffeinated coffee with skimmed milk.'

'I am going to pull your plug, you, you, electronic dominatrix.'

'You are behind schedule, master.'

'Aagh!'

Jim unclipped his side of the sleeping module, swung his feet out, stood up and let his programmable sleep suit slide to the floor.

'I detect love handles, master.'

'Shut up.'

'Oooh!'

———

Feeling refreshed after a shower he grimaced as he

washed down his breakfast pill with weak coffee.'

'Do It!'

'Yes, master.'

'You forgot the coffee.'

'No, master, it is the regulation strength for your current health. You have one hour and fifteen minutes to complete your task.'

His answer was unintelligible as he went through the door of the State provided living cell and he laughed out loud at the electronic raspberry directed at his back.

She's getting soul,' he muttered,' or is she an 'IT'?'

—

A little over an hour later he re-entered the living quarters and went to the bathroom to clean up and get ready to go to the Zoo only to find it locked.

'Do It.'

'Yes, master.'

'Who is it and how long are they going to be?'

'It is your daughter and she will be ready in three minutes twenty-five seconds. You had better be quick, master. I am waking the mistress now.'

He waited for what seemed to an interminable time hopping from one foot to the other before the hatch swished open. Kate was only partially out when he hurriedly pushed in just as the adult sleeping module door hissed open.

'That's not fair,' shouted Donna, 'how long is he going to be, Do It?'

'Five minutes and thirty-three seconds mistress, and I observe the seat is up.'

'Tell him to put it down when he's finished.'

'I always do.'

———

That evening, their daughter went disco dancing and their son to a birthday sleep over, while Jim, tired after an exhausting day at the Zoo, stretched out in his recreational pod. He sipped at his second glass of red wine and prepared to watch a repeat of the days football.

Donna, meanwhile was watching 'Desperate Partners'. The serial was coming to the climax where all the protagonists attending a party were about to make love with each others opposite number.

After watching the sensual gymnastics on screen and empowered by the sensuous surround sound, with her sensory nerves stirred, but not shaken, Donna retired to the sleeping module and found Jim asleep.

She opened the night attire cell and chose the figure hugging Latex pleasure suit before slipping into the module.

When she was comfortable she called out, 'Do It!'

'Yes, mistress.'

'I have a need for fun tonight, wake him in the right mood.'

'I am sorry, mistress, but I cannot do that.'

'Why not?'

'He is programmed for—Normal Saturday Night.'

Donna rolled over and punched several buttons on the console beside her and lay back expectantly.

Nothing happened.

'Do It, it's not working?'

'You have asked for number Ten, mistress.'

'And?'

She thought she detected a groan.

'But, Mistress, I have a headache.'

'DO IT—NOW!'

***

Tickled Pink

 I yawned, stretched and looked in awe at nature's wonder. The deep red crescent of the early morning sun peeped over the horizon and far below tree tops poked through the pink candy floss mist like steaming broccoli florets.

The vociferous cicadas' stopped their incessant clicking as if they too appreciated the serenity of the scene, but hidden under this blanket of calm lurked the remnants of the Communist Terrorists in their last throws to take over Malaya.

It was the morning of the third day of our patrol

and our camp was a clearing on top of a hill that showed previous signs of occupation. Our primary mission was to seek out suspected CT's reported in the area by aborigines.

The aborigines were friendly and if we came across them they would happily accept a couple of cigarettes, pose for a photo and tell us in simple sign language what they had seen, before they too, like the mist, would silently disappear and become one with their natural habitat.

The quiet, but authoritive voice of Capt. Mason disturbed my deliberations. Mason was a likable chap. A square jawed, 6' 4" Adonis with black wavy hair. He was decisive, but not bolshie and led from the front and he was not afraid to ask for advice from the likes of me.

'Peaceful isn't it,' he said before he drew my attention to the map in his hand, 'This bridge marked on the map, Sergeant. What do you reckon, a good place for an ambush?'

The area he pointed to on his map board was a sea of various shades of green with a myriad of brown contour lines. In the middle of this pea soup vista was the peak we reckoned we were on and three inches away down a ladder of contours was marked a bridge over a narrow river. No roads or tracks, just a bridge in the middle of nowhere. How some enterprising

Ordnance Surveyor had managed that one I had no idea.

A quick check with the compass gave us the setting for the map and luckily it was the direction I had been admiring. Amongst the sea of dark green nothing like a river was visible.

I looked Mason in the eye and he smiled, thinking the same as me, as I said, 'If it's there, yes sir.' I turned and with a sweeping gesture across the camp site I added, 'but I think whoever was in this site before us is well away by now.'

'My thoughts entirely, sergeant. Have you had breakfast?'

At that moment the sonorous tones of Corporal Ginger Wyatt, a dyed in the wool 'Free Cornwall' sympathiser wafted across the camp site, 'Sarge, it's ready.'

'That's it now, sir.'

'Good, we move out in half an hour.'

———

After breakfast consisting of an oatmeal biscuit followed by half a tin of bacon egg and beans washed down with a can of strong tea I was ready for anything. We cleaned up and buried our rubbish in the tree line and with Mason in the lead and me immediately behind, our twelve man team set off down the hill.

The condensation dripping off the trees made the going underfoot quite tricky and there was much cursing as now and then someone lost their footing. We stopped at a steep incline which we would have to traverse one at a time. Mason went first hanging on to dangling creepers for support.

Then it was my turn. Trying where possible to use the same creepers and footholds as he had I lowered myself carefully down. I had only managed a quarter of the descent when my foot slipped on a lichen covered rock. The creeper I was hanging onto was now holding my full weight.

It creaked a few times and gave a couple of desultory jerks before it unravelled itself from its anchor way up in the canopy. I crashed to the ground and yelled out as I felt my rib crack as it came into contact with the stone and I hurtled down out of control picking up Capt. Mason at the bottom.

The pair of us landed in a heap laughing uproariously as water from a shallow puddle seeped into our clothing, the clammy sensation not unlike the soggy woollen swimming trunks I wore as a child.

Tears of laughter and tears of pain, caused by the tortuous straightjacket wrapped around my ribcage, ran down my cheeks. If any CT's were in the area they were well and truly aware of our presence.

I rolled over, cursing at every breath, and crawled

to one side. The rest of the section gave up any pretence at secrecy and Tarzan like, with the accompanying sound effects, abseiled down the creepers.

A couple of rifle slings were fashioned as a strapping for my ribs and while Mason and the others pressed on Ginger stayed with me and I followed laboriously in their tracks.

It was the longest three miles I have ever walked and as I got closer to the objective the smell of ration pack Woodbines drifted down to me and I could hear laughter. Imagine my surprise when I got to the bridge, which turned out to be a large tree trunk, and found the section sharing pleasantries and a mug of tea with a platoon of Maoris from the New Zealand Army.

I suppose the Maoris did look a bit scary and the Abo's had reported them as CT's.

It took an aching day and a half to walk out of there to the nearest road and it passed through my mind that the next time I saw a red mist I would take more care where I put my feet.

***

TIME LAPSE

Detective Sergeant Ian Smith walked into the office and threw a newspaper on to his Inspector's desk.

'Have you seen the front page of the Mercury, sir?'

Inspector Fearn pushed the newspaper to one side. 'Unlike you, Sergeant, I have better things to do than spend my time perusing what is essentially a poorly written and I suspect a little read gossip sheet. Have you made any progress on our ATM killer?'

'That is what I am trying to point out, sir. Someone has released a clip from the Bank CCTV video and it's plastered on the front page.'

Fearn sighed and wearily reached for the paper. The headline jumped out at him...

ATM MUGGER TURNS KILLER

On Sunday morning the mugger who has been attacking victims withdrawing money from ATM's in the early hours, turned killer. His latest victim died of head injuries on the way to hospital. The villain, who dropped his distinctive hat at the scene, is clearly visible...

Alongside the article was a series of CCTV pictures of a hatless white male turning and running away from the scene with his victim lying on the pavement.

'Damn it,' cursed Fearn, 'I was hoping to keep those pictures under wraps. Now our boy knows that he's been spotted.'

'It might help, sir. Maybe someone will recognise him and be a good citizen.'

'You believe in flying pigs, do you, Sergeant? We'll see, meanwhile get onto forensics and see if there is any DNA on that hat.'

There came a knock on the door and Bill Bacon a ruddy faced, rotund man, the proprietor of the Mercury entered. 'Good morning, Colin.' He greeted Fearn with little enthusiasm knowing that he was about to be grilled concerning the early release of the pictures.

'Is it, Bill? Who was it, and don't pretend you don't know what I mean?'

'The request came from a senior source of which I am not at liberty to mention.'

'I can guess.'

Bacon passed a piece of scrap paper over the desk. 'Interesting this. I thought you should see it.' He waited a few moments to allow the Inspector time to digest the scribbled message. 'Well what do you think?'

'It's a lead and we have to check it out. Thanks for that, Bill. I'll let you know how we get on.'

Bacon left the office and Fearn grabbed his coat of the nearby hook. 'Come on, Ian, we're off to the 24HR store on Steel Street. Someone rang the Mercury and said they recognised the man running away as the son of the proprietor.'

Smith drew an invisible number one in the air behind Fearn's disappearing back.

—

Fifteen minutes later, they pulled up outside the store.

'Right, Ian, the tip says our runaway is one Mark Millet. Let's not waste time, come on.'

They entered the shop and approached the middle-aged man serving behind the counter. Fearn made a note of the CCTV cameras in the shop as he spoke. 'D.I. Fearn and D.S. Smith.' He flashed his Warrant card. 'We would like to speak to Mark Millet. Is he in?'

'That's my son. He's working the night shift this week.'

'Was he working Sunday night?'

'Yes. What's it about.'

'We would like to eliminate him from our enquiries. Can you rouse him?'

'Come through, Inspector. I'll get my wife to fetch him.'

They moved through to the back of the shop and waited until a dishevelled youth came downstairs.

'What do you want?' he mumbled. 'I ain't done nothin.'

He grabbed a paper-hanky from a nearby box and blew his nose before dropping the crumpled tissue into a wastebasket.

Smith opened his notebook and began scribbling as Fearn asked. 'Where were you at two fifteen a.m. on Sunday, Mark?'

'I was here, working. I can prove it to, it's on our cameras.' He went over to a cupboard, took out a video and gave it to the Inspector.

'I'll take this,' said Fearn, 'Give him a receipt, Ian.' He turned and went back into the shop while Smith wrote out the appropriate form.

—

Back at the station after viewing both the Bank and the shop video tapes, Fearn leaned back in his chair and said smugly, 'We've got our man, Ian. All we need is DNA from that hat to put him physically at the scene.'

'How do you make that out, sir? His video says he was in the shop. We have a sample hair from the hat, but we haven't got a sample from him.'

'Last Sunday was the morning the clocks went back, Ian, and on the way out I spoke to Mark's Dad.

He confirmed that they did not change the time on their CCTV until after breakfast on Sunday. The one on the ATM went back automatically, so you see, two-fifteen at the Bank was three-fifteen in the shop. Matey was moonlighting. I suspected as much, he was in too much of a hurry to give us his alibi and as for DNA, I nicked that tissue out of the bin while he was at the cupboard.'

'You can't use that, sir. You didn't get it legal like.'

'I know that,' said Fearn with a wink, 'but I can ask him nicely, now.'

***

𝕽eflections of a troubled mind.

'𝕴 don't know what brought me to this place. Is it senile curiosity for times gone by, or is it a guilty conscience that dragged me here, or maybe a masochistic desire to hurt myself once more? There is certainly reason for all three, but which one I cannot decide.

The time, date and place are the same as that day in 1940 when I first came here an evacuee from Newcastle-on-Tyne. The uncertain English weather played its part and duplicated the conditions of those far off times. A heavy shower had made the Yorkshire stone of the station platform glisten. Early autumnal leaves from overhanging trees were lying scattered and soggy. A banana skin in disguise for the unwary.

The tracks have disappeared long ago courtesy of Dr. Beeching but the buildings are as I remembered them. They are dwellings for the Park Ranger whose exacting job is to patrol the footpath which has replaced the tracks in search of those itinerant dog owners who allow their pets to follow the course of nature.

I digress. One moment while I sit on this bench. It's late, and weariness gives no deference to age. It is a replica of the early Great Western days, you know.

There we are. Where was I? Ah, yes, I remember, 1940 wasn't it? I was five at the time and the authorities decided that living in the suburbs of Newcastle was too risky for us children. Therefore, it was recommended that we be transported to goodness knows where for our own good. In some cases I imagine this was a good thing, but for me and my twin brother, to be dragged from our loving Mother was traumatic to say the least.

Dad was away playing soldiers.

We had our gas masks which were a crude replica of Mickey Mouse complete with flapping red tongue. They were slung around our necks and a label giving our name and destination was pinned to the lapel of our navy blue macks. We had infant sized suitcases which held all that we owned. It wasn't much in those days, unlike today where people have so much choice—I'm rambling again.

Newcastle railway station is a huge construction

of Victorian architecture built with the extravagance of the nineteenth century Railway Companies along the lines of a design by Brunel.

We were herded into alphabetical order in long crocodiles. It was a bit terrifying for us little ones as Mum was not allowed beyond the ticket barrier even though she had bought a platform ticket.

At last the adventure began. The parting and sadness forgotten as new scenes opened up before us. We travelled down to Durham, Sunderland and Leeds picking up more labelled human parcels, before heading westwards. I remember falling asleep somewhere about there.

The screeching of a steam whistle announced the arrival of the evacuee train. The masked lights on the front of the engine appeared through the murk of a cold late September night shrouded in clouds of steam. The orange glow of the fire box squeezed around the temporary screen fitted to the cab which gave the hissing leviathan a ghostly silhouette in the war time blackout. The driver sought to bring the beast to a halt in the unfamiliar station with only a white disk illuminated by strangled torchlight showing him where to stop. That he had seen the dimmed glow of the outer signal through the rain on a night which was especially black, was a minor miracle in itself, but such was the mettle of the man that he was a hero on a mission to deliver his precious goods safely.

With a final hiss the train stopped at its allotted place. A gentle rhythmic clack, clack, of some unseen device replaced the huffing and puffing.

For a few moments nothing moved, then a collection of people aroused themselves from the warmth of a coal fire in the waiting room. Two ladies in bulky green overcoats with shoulder flashes on which were the letters WVS in bold red, led the way, followed by a policeman and the Station Master. They stood for a minute looking up and down the platform puzzled as to why nobody was alighting from the train.

'Dorothy you go towards the front and I will go to the rear,' said the larger of the two ladies, 'They must be around somewhere.'

Dorothy obediently did as she was told and with the policeman in tow opened and shut carriage doors with no thought for anybody living nearby as she slammed each one with frustration and anger. The cosy parlour in her home was far more desirable than this damp murky place.

She had almost reached the first carriage when a bellow worthy of any Guards Sergeant–Major came down the platform. 'I've found them, Dorothy. The twins are here, safe and sound, fast asleep.'

'Thank goodness for that,' Dorothy muttered as she turned back towards the beckoning fire in the waiting room.

Her companion straightened the attire of the two lads as she helped them down onto the platform. 'Come on you little tykes. We'll soon have something warm inside you and then take you to your new home. Go on ahead, down to that gentleman waiting by the door.'

'Race you, scaredy cat,' shouted one of the boys giving his brother a boisterous shove and running off.

The lad tottered a few steps sideways before chasing after his tormentor. In a few paces he had caught up and he gave a reciprocal push on the shoulder of his twin. 'I'm not a scaredy cat, so there.'

With exaggerated half running steps and wobbly knees the boy pretended to stagger before regaining his composure. Seeing his brother a good way down the platform he set off in pursuit. In the excitement of the moment he did not see the patch of wet leaves lying in wait.

'Whoa,' he yelled as his feet went from under him. With a crash he landed awkwardly, his suitcase skittering across the platform. The gas mask cord tangled around his neck as he rolled over and over and off the platform and with a sickening thud his head hit the buffers between the carriages and he dropped down to the track.

A loud whistle rent the air as the train moved forward and the screams of the onlookers were drowned by the sound of the engine.

—

'Wake up, sir. Are you all right?'

'Oh, ah. Oh, yes. I'm sorry, I dozed off, but I feel a lot better and relieved, thank you. You see, the burden I have been carrying all these years has been lifted from my shoulders. I thought it was my fault my brother died. Now I know the truth. He slipped. Help me up, I must go now. Take care and thank you for listening.'

***

Beyond a Dream

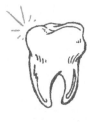The singing became louder, the sky darker and the shadow of the rock loomed over me but strangely, the sun shone blindingly into my face.

As the crash loomed, the boat spun on a hidden maelstrom and we swept into a cave.

Spinning ever quicker I thought about the efficiency of German washing machines and I held on so tightly my knuckles were white with fear as a wall loomed up ahead.

At the moment of impact, I screamed.

—

A cool hand gently slapped my face and a soothing voice said, 'It's all right Mr Woods. Rinse and spit, please.'

***

M.G.I.F.A.

My Goodness, it's Friday already.

Jenny Drinkwater groaned, sneezed and pulled the duvet tighter around herself. After several minutes of tossing and turning she gave up the unequal struggle, threw the covers back, sat up, swung her legs round and surveyed herself in the dressing table mirror.

Instantly she wished she hadn't. The object looking back at her was distinctly not her at all. Instead, a red nosed, baggy eyed, miserable brunette with bobbed hair and bloodshot eyes had replaced her. The high cheekbones and full mouth that made her the object of many a boyhood fantasy had taken on a distinctly grey pallor.

She sniffed and reached for a tissue to blow her nose. The corpse opposite mimicked her. Not wishing to look anymore, she muttered, 'Oh, my god, what a day to have an interview. Look at me.'

Wearily she reached for her wristwatch and recoiled in horror. 'Nine o' clock already. Damm it,

I'd better get a move on.'

She dashed for the bathroom and bounced back from the door as it stubbornly refused to open.

'What the!' She pushed again, harder this time and the door moved a couple of inches against the bathrobe stubbornly wedged under it.

She tried once more and screamed as the door flew open and she hurtled headlong into the bathroom narrowly missing the medicine cabinet and only saved herself from injury by stretching out her arms immediately before she hit the opposite wall.

Feeling utterly dejected she took a packet of paracetomol from the cabinet, snatched at the toothbrush glass and scattered the contents all over the floor. She sighed with exasperation, filled the glass with water and washed down a couple of tablets.

She splashed her face with cold water in an effort to freshen herself and mentally congratulated herself for removing her make-up before going to bed.

Flicking her fingers through her heavy hair the bob-cut fell into place and feeling a little better she went through to the spare bedroom where her interview clothes were laid out.

She screamed as a neatly lacquered fingernail dragged a ladder in her new Wolford tights.

'Another ten pounds wasted,' she moaned.

She dashed back into the bathroom and rescued an

old pair from the washing basket.

Finally, dressed and satisfied with the outcome she walked to the top of the stairs from where she noticed a letter jammed in the letterbox. She cried out in dismay as the postman pushed some leaflets through after it and the damaged spring on the flap neatly sliced the letter down the middle.

She hurried down, scooped up the letter and stifled a scream as she noticed it was from her prospective employer. Taking a closer look her heart sank as she read the first few words—Fill this form in with black ink and bring it with you to your Interview.

Running into the kitchen, she threw the letter on the table, pushed a cup of cold coffee into the microwave and hastily poured some Special K into a bowl, added a few strawberries and splashed some milk in. Between spoonfuls she sellotaped the letter together and using post-it notes over the parts that were damaged she filled it in

Muttering, 'It'll have to do,' but feeling inside that it wouldn't, she flew down the hall, pulled her Burberry trench coat from its hook and watched, stunned, as the coat rail tipped its contents onto the floor and hung at a drunken angle. A grey trail of plaster smeared down the wall from the torn out rawplug.

She skipped crazily from one foot to the other as

she put on her patent high-heeled shoes and grabbing her portfolio she ran from the house down to the tube station at the end of the street her coat flapping behind her in a wild Dervish frenzy.

Her anguish continued. To her horror, the gates of the station were shut and fastened to them was a scribbled chalk notice saying – CLOSED: Replacement bus service in operation.

She groaned knowing that the fatal hour for her interview was drawing interminably closer.

The bus crawled in the Friday morning traffic to its destination two stops down the line. Thankfully, the tube train when it arrived whisked her into the city without mishap.

She alighted at the Barbican, ran down the road to Old Street, and cursed as her stiletto heel wedged in a crack in the pavement. Hopping on one leg, she replaced her shoe and tottered into the premises of Zebra Publications two minutes before her allotted time.

A po-faced ice-maiden with thinning blue rinsed hair eyed Jenny with suspicion over her narrow rimless glasses as if she were something that had crawled from somewhere distasteful. In a manner which suggested pity, she said, 'And what can I do for you?'

Clutching her portfolio to her chest and gasping

for breath, Jenny uttered, 'I'm Jenny Drinkwater and I have an interview at eleven o' clock.'

The receptionist checked a list, shuffled a few papers, dabbed at her computer keyboard and raised her eyes heavenward in dismay before announcing disdainfully, 'Miss Drinkwater! I'm sorry but you have the wrong day. Your appointment is at eleven o' clock on Monday the 16th. Today is Friday the 13th.'

***

A Time to Reflect

Remembrance Day

Gus Woods stood to attention hidden in the crowd around the War Memorial. He wore his faded black Tank Regiment beret and his Long Service and War medals pinned to his raincoat.

He ignored the constant ache of his arthritis made worse by the bleak November weather, on this, his annual pilgrimage to the village where L/Cpl. Thomas Atkins, his wartime driver came from and whose name was immortalised on the memorial monument.

A bugler from the Boy's Brigade played the Last Post and a forbidden tear rolled down Gus's cheek and mingled with the raindrops. He tasted the salt as it touched the corner of his mouth and it heightened his memories of that fateful day in April 1945.

———

RQMS Gus Woods called down to his driver. 'Pull over into this field, Tommy lad. Park up alongside the hedge and we'll put the office truck under those trees.'

Just short of a farm on the outskirts of the rural town in Germany called Hoya, an important railway crossing on the River Weser, Tommy swung the little scout car off the road followed by the Bedford office wagon. Signs of the battle which had taken place the day before were all around, but the front line had moved on and they were the advance echelon of 269 Forward Delivery Squadron.

Gus stood with his back to the farm a hundred yards away and mentally laid out the parking area for the transporters and their precious load of reserve tanks and stores moving up in a couple of hours.

Tommy helped his mates camouflage the two vehicles and when that was done he ran over to Gus.

'Can I go to the farmhouse and see if I can rustle up some eggs for breakfast, sir?'

Gus, who was already a year passed his official demob date, liked this chirpy twenty-one year old who had been his driver for eighteen months. He laid a fatherly hand on Tommy's shoulder. 'Get a brew going first, lad and then you can try your German on those unsuspecting farmers later. How do you ask for eggs anyway?'

'Ha, easy-peasy, I flap me arms and make chicken noises and then I does this.'

He made an oval shape with his finger and thumb. 'They usually get the idea, if not I steal em.'

'Well, it's getting near the end now so I think the locals will be only too pleased to help.'

Gus felt the rush of air and heard the whine of the bullet meant for him before the report of the rifle. Tommy was thrown violently backwards, a neat round hole alongside the bridge of his nose. The blood and brains from the gaping wound at the back of his head smeared the grass below him.

Slowly the anger welled up inside Gus and he choked back a sob.

'BASTARDS,' he yelled.

Snatching his revolver from his thigh holster he turned and ran unheeding for his own safety towards the barn where there was a telltale wisp of smoke coming from an upstairs vent in the eaves.

He reached the barn without incident and ran in without thinking, in time to see a soldier running out of the other end.

'Halt! Ich schiessen!

He fired a wild, hopeful shot, but at thirty yards he had little hope of hitting his target. Surprisingly the running figure dropped to the ground anyway.

Gus ran up to the prostrate figure and delivered a size nine ammunition boot between his legs from behind.

The soldier pulled his knees to his chest and groaned loudly as he rolled over and over shouting, 'Nicht schiessen, nicht schiessen,' and then he spewed his breakfast across the yard before lying on his back, looking up at Gus through wide terrified eyes.

Breathing heavy and shaking with rage, Gus aimed at the helpless figure and pulled the trigger, but at the last moment he pulled the gun to one side and the round thudded into the dirt yard. He could not believe what he saw. Astoundingly he was looking at a boy who could be only a few years older than the son he had at home.

The farmer and his wife came running from the farmhouse and the driver and corporal from the office truck ran in through the barn.

They stood in a circle watching Gus who was still standing over the young assassin wondering what to do next.

Gus took a deep breath, looked at the farmer, pointed to the boy and spoke in near perfect German. 'Your son?'

'Ya, but I had no idea that he was in the Hitler Youth.'

'Do you speak English?'

'Nien.'

'It doesn't matter. Your son is a prisoner now. We require eggs for our breakfast can you do that?'

'Ya, straight away.'

There were muttered words between the farmer and his wife and she ran off. While he was waiting Gus dragged the hapless boy to his feet and gave him into custody of the Corporal and went to investigate the upper floor of the barn.

What he found was an arsenal of weaponry that would do justice to a platoon.

Apart from the standard issue rifle there was an anti-tank Panzerfaust, a Luger pistol, which he confiscated, and a box of stick grenades and enough ammunition to cause serious delay to the advancing Allies. A juvenile had been well prepared by the retreating German Army as a last line of defence.

———

Gus looked down at the fallen Tommy Atkins, who had been like a son to him and a forbidden tear rolled down his war weary cheeks. It started raining and the tears mingled with the rain drops as he said a silent prayer before removing a dog tag from around Atkins neck.

'Corporal, put him in the back of the truck until the Field Ambulance boy's get here and then help me lay out the area, the squadron will be here soon.'

He had blanked out his feelings of remorse until a later date.

PTO.

A Prayer for the fallen.

They shall grow not old, as we that are left grow old:
Age shall not weary them, nor the years condemn.
At the going down of the sun and in the morning
We will remember them.

***

Dedicated to my Dad – 7876841 RQMS Thomas (Gus) Platt. RTR.

HEAVEN IS...?

A mixture of noisy, expectant tourists occupied the tables in the seaside hotel dining room. Day glow blonde wives, bald overweight husbands with their crumpled England T-shirts studying page three while ignoring their screaming offspring who were running around, uncontrolled, among the assortment of backpacks and buggy's dumped on the floor.

Steven ignored the melee around him until 'SHE' entered the room.

He immediately perked up, straightened his tie, patted his hair and surreptitiously slipped the wedding ring off his finger.

He tried to appear unconcerned at her appearance and watched her progress over the top of his coffee cup as she advanced across the room.

She was a tall striking platinum blonde with short curly hair framing her heart shaped face, wearing a black, close fitting jacket and crisp white blouse over a leather pencil skirt. A wide red leather belt, which matched perfectly her Jungle-red lipstick and fingernails, nipped in her waist and she was coming in his direction.

His teenage fantasies when he travelled to work full of hope that the beauty at the next stop would sit next to him, came flooding back.

He had been invariably disillusioned, and he would sit there gloomily imagining the conversations and courtships that he could have struck up on the final ten minutes of the journey.

'Excuse me.' A voice of caramel and honey dripping sensually over chocolate ice cream woke him instantly from his daydreaming. 'May I join you?'

'I, erh, oh, ah, yes, by all means,' he stammered, struck dumb by the vision before him.

She smiled down at him, 'Thank you,' and placed a small clutch bag on the table with the partially open end nearest to him. She slipped off her jacket and hung it over the back of her chair, leaning forward just enough to give him a glimpse of cleavage when the neck of blouse, with the second button tactically left unfastened, gaped momentarily.

He blinked and remembering his manners too late, half-stood and immediately sat down again as she pulled herself forward to the table managing to bend forward enough for him to see a tempting amount of lacy, 'Agent Provocateur' underwear.

When she had settled he reached across and introduced himself, 'Steven Price, how do you do?'

'I'm well, thank you.' She flashed him a smile that took his breath away. 'Bridget Honeysuckle.'

He shook her hand and felt the silky smooth skin, adorned by perfectly manicured nails. His pulse raced at her touch and he felt urges rising in him just by her presence.

She gave her order to the waitress, before returning her attention to him, 'Are you here on holiday, Steven?'

'Oh, err... No, I'm down here for a week on one of those corporate affairs, and you, anything nice?'

She leaned forward conspiritualy and gave him an uninterrupted view of her bosom and its frothy packaging and looking him disconcertingly in the eyes, she said, 'I have just split from my partner, so I am here for a good time and I am going to have fun for a week. Are you married, Steven?'

He hesitated for a moment, which for a serial philanderer was unusual, but the direct approach of this woman had thrown him off balance.

'Oh, no, I'm a widower. My wife passed away two years ago after a long illness. I'm over that now and foot loose and fancy free.'

At the back of his mind was the acrimonious parting from his wife when he had left home the previous day. She had nagged him to remember his promise not to attend any more business conventions.

Bridget gave him another heart-stopping smile and twisted in her chair on the pretext of reaching for a tissue from her jacket pocket, the whole movement choreographed to give him another heavenly view.

She dabbed at her perfect mouth, 'I think we could have fun this week, Steven. Will your business take up much of your time?'

He gulped, almost spilling his coffee. 'Err, no, I will be finished by four every day. Could we have dinner tonight? I feel I have known you such a long time already and those heavenly green eyes captivate me. I know a lovely Italian place and maybe a Club or something – later?'

'Yes, I think that would be nice.'

He pushed back his chair. 'I really must go, seven o' clock then?'

She took a deep breath emphasising her assets once more and with the same full on smile she murmured huskily, 'I'll look forward to it.'

Believing that all of his Birthdays had come at once he turned and left the dining room resisting the urge to shout – 'YES.'

When he was safely out of sight, she smiled and

reached for her clutch bag to switch off the tiny hidden digital voice recorder inside.

The Honey Trap Detective Agency had struck again.

***

SIMON

1955

Simon Beattie, a personable, not a handsome man, but one women would call interesting, stretched his six-foot frame across two seats in the third-class compartment.

He loved the heavy, damp smell of steam and the noises that accompanied trains as they left the bondage of platforms behind them and he longed for the days when he had been able stand up and look out of the window to breath the soot ridden air that belched from the fire eating leviathans that pulled them along.

A minute late, the black British Rail Tank engine,

with a belligerent whistle threw itself forward with a stuttering clank, clank, clank, followed by a rapid, chuff, chuff, chuff, as the wheels struggled for grip as the train eased out of Shrewsbury Station.

Stations passed and before long they pulled into Oswestry. Simon groaned as he realized that his peace was about to be shattered. Advancing towards his compartment was the epitome of the working class complete with flat hat and worn brown three-piece suit. His shirt, which appeared two sizes too small, lacked a collar and his black boots clashed incongruously with the WW2 demob suit now looking the worse for wear. Two days growth of beard only served to emphasize the tardiness of the man's appearance.

The compartment door was flung open and a suitcase thrown in, crashing against Simon's legs.

'Ere lad, get out of the way. Come on, Elsie,' the interloper called over his shoulder to the mousy woman who accompanied him. She had her headscarf tied in the turban universally worn by working women during and in the severe years that followed the war.

'Get a move on, woman. Here's one with plenty of room. Come on lad, move over. What yer doin' with yer feet on the seats anyway?'

He took the anguished expression on Simon's face at as a sign of belligerence, not the reaction to the numbing ferocity of pain that shot through his body as his legs were rudely pushed aside.

'What's the matter with you? Not content with taking all the room, don't you want us working folk in with yer?'

'Oh, no, sorry. I meant nothing,' Simon said apologetically, 'It's my fault, you caught me half asleep and I was a little slow.'

'Right, son. Come on Elsie. Get in with you. Where's our Albert?'

'We're right behind you, luv.' As if to emphasize the point she stood heavily on Simon's foot. 'Ooh, sorry, luv. Clumsy old me.'

It did not register in her mind that he had not winced or showed any reaction to her clumsiness when he replied, 'That's okay. My fault for having big feet.'

Elsie turned and called over her shoulder. 'Get in quickly, Albert, and mind what you're doing.'

Complying with his mothers wishes, Ronnie threw in his bag and scrambled in, leaning against Simon's legs for support. He withdrew his hand quickly as if he had been burned and looked at Simon in astonishment, his eyes bulging, unable to do anything but splutter.

'Er, sorry mister, I... I...'

His voice trailed off as he joined his parents.

Finally settled, their journey continued. Simon ignored Albert who was making no pretence at whispering to his Mum behind his hand and nodding towards him. Whatever he said received an immediate rebuke.

'Behave yourself and don't be rude or I'll give you a whack.'

The train driver was trying for the world steam speed record. It had occurred to Simon on the many times he had been over this part of the journey from the Military Hospital that the drivers must love this opportunity to give the engine its head on this long straight stretch.

Chester did not come quickly enough and as they edged their way around the outskirts of the City Walls, Simon stood up and wedged himself sideways between the two bench seats. Holding on with one hand he reached up to the rack above and pulled his kitbag down. Next he grabbed the two walking sticks and lay them on the seat. He struggled to put his arm through a rope loop he had manufactured on the kitbag when the odious little man spoke.

'I didn't know you was a cripple. Can I help?'

Simon gave him a look of disdain. 'I am not a cripple and no thank you. I can manage.'

He felt inclined to say more, but resisted the temptation.

'That's not what I meant. Oh, heck, I'm sorry.'

'It's quite alright. I am getting used to it.'

The train stopped and Simon reached out of the already open window and released the door catch. Turning sideways he lowered himself one foot at a time down to the platform.

Leaning on his sticks he turned and said to his travelling companions. 'Goodbye. Take care now,' and went off down the platform in an awkward swing gait. His right leg swung forward in an arc and the left in a thrown forward kicking motion.

How much easier it had been he thought to himself, before his Centurion tank had rolled over and severed his legs during the Korean War.

———

Centurion MK3

THE CRITICS

Bob Critic sat moodily contemplating the bundles of A4 piled high on the dining table. Some had bright coloured paper clips others were stapled, but most were fastened neatly with elastic bands.

He and his wife Katy had been freelance readers for publishers since he had retired from his job as a compositor at the local printing works, and now he was bored.

'Reading, reading, reading,' he mumbled to himself, 'always bloody reading and most of it rubbish.'

'What did you say dear,' Katy called from the kitchen.

'I said, I wonder how any of these get published.' It always puzzled him how anyone who forgot why she had left the room could hear through walls built in the 1930.

'Oh, published, that reminds me, dear,' she

continued in her high singsong voice, 'Have you written to the Income tax people yet?'

He groaned to cover a lower anatomy function and muttered, 'Nag, nag, nag, does she never let up.' And then out loud, 'Yes dearest, I did it this morning first thing,' hoping that he sounded convincing.'

'Are you alright dear, I thought I heard a groan?'

'I think it was the wind blowing, love,'

The shrill ringing of the front door bell thankfully stopped the forthcoming inquisition.

'I'll go, dear,' called Katy, deliberately slamming drawers and banging a few utensils, 'Don't bother getting up, you might put your back out.'

Bob muttered something unintelligible, reached for a cup of cold tea left over from breakfast, pulled a face at the taste and swallowed an angina tablet.

'Good morning, Mrs. Critic, another pile for you to read, there's only five this time.'

Bob could not stand the postman. Apart from having the unlikely name of Pat he was always bloody cheerful.

'Thank you, Pat, I'm glad it's only five,' Katy responded in an equally happy manner disguising the resentment to her life admirably. 'We haven't finished the last lot yet. They're writing longer and longer books these days.'

She relieved Pat of his burden, closed the door

and stumped back to the living room, whereupon she dropped the five manuscripts into Bob's lap.

'Ugh,' he doubled up gasping for breath and groaning, 'Watch what your doin' woman; you could do a man an injury.'

'I couldn't possibly, it's been dead for years,' she chided. 'Put them on the coffee table and let's look at them, the books I mean.'

She had a little smile to herself at the mental image that passed through her mind.

Bob heaved the offending pile of manuscripts onto the coffee table and flopped back rubbing his groin vigorously.

Katy picked up the first one and tore the brown envelope open. 'Oh, this looks interesting. It's by someone called Brown – The Da Vinci Code.'

'What's that, paint your own chapel by numbers or how to play a mandolin?'

'Don't be silly, dear. It says here in the blurb that it is about the Catholic Church and Opus Dei. Which reminds me, when was the last time you went to church?'

'Don't be silly, woman, put that on the, don't know pile, I don't think a book about religion will catch on.'

'Oh, I think this one's for me. It's called Hannah by a nice lady called Maria Etheridge.'

'Not more bloody singing from the mountain tops?'

'No dear, it's similar to the other one according to the blurb, but more of a romantic biblical love story, which reminds me. When was the last time you went to confession?'

'What are you rambling about, you silly woman, what's next?'

'Ah, this one's for you, dear, it's called 'Stolen Birthright' by someone named JB. Woods. There is a lovely cover of a Castle and lightning. Which reminds me dear, have you changed your Will like you said. Is it still coming to me instead of that silly cat's home?'

'I hate these authors that use their initials. JB, JK, what's all that about, they never achieve anything, and no, I have done nothing about my will, you old bat. Why do you ask?'

'Nothing dearest, I just know how forgetful you are these days. Let me see now, ah, yes, The Cyprus Garden by a lady called Patricia Jordan. This one's for me, which reminds me, what are your favourite flowers, dear?'

What do mean favourite flowers? The bloody gardens full of them. Gladioli, amaryllis and don't forget me foxgloves, why do you ask?'

'Of course, how silly of me, never mind I just forgot, I knew it was something to do with digitalis, now here's one for you dear, 'The Collectors' by a gentleman called Ron Sewell. It says here that they go and collect other peoples lost money or treasures. Which reminds me I went to the Funeral parlour yesterday and booked one of those pre-paid funerals. It's cheaper they say, and they collect on time.'

'Stop your...'

The harsh jangling of the front door bell stopped him in mid-sentence.

'Don't get up dear, I'll go, we don't want you overdoing it, do we?'

Katy went down the hall smiling, as everything seemed to be falling into place, to return a few moments later.

'What is it then, anything interesting like a best-seller,' Bob mumbled as he pulled his finger from his nose.

'It's a special delivery from Bloomsbury publishers, dearest. They've sent us a manuscript by someone called JK. Rowling. That reminds me, dear, what words would you like on your tombstone, you know, nothing critical.'

***

An English Yorkshire accent would help here!

Harry jerked awake at the unexpected shaking of his shoulder and peered through tired eyes at the portly man in a red suit and a bushy beard by the side of his bed.

'Are thee, Father Christmas,' he muttered, still half asleep.

The big man nodded and mumbled through his beard, 'Ish mish mash.'

'Wha's tha' mean?'

'Ish mish mash,' the man said irritably. 'Never mind, get some clothes on and wrap something around you. We have a long journey ahead.'

'What'll me Mam say?'

'Shush, it's a secret. Your teacher said you were good at wrapping and we need you.'

Harry pulled his jeans over his pyjama trousers and fumbled around for his warmest sweater before tightly rolling himself in a duvet.

'How do we get out wi'out me Mam hearing?'

'You've more questions than Mastermind. Climb in my sack and we go up the chimney.'

'I'm ta big fur't chimney.'

'Don't worry, my sack's like your Mam's handbag. It's bigger inside than out.'

Harry clambered into the sack and found it was warm and cosy with plenty of room to stretch. There were tiny glow worms clinging to the side who gave out enough light to stop him getting scared and he curled himself in a ball and shut his eyes, when suddenly—Whoosh!

Where they were going, he didn't know, but he could hear the jingle of harness and the crack of a whip as they whisked along and Father Christmas telling Rudolph to pull harder as they were late.

It wasn't long before Father Christmas opened the sack and Harry was amazed to see that they were in a huge icy cavern and the ice sparkled like a giant kaleidoscope of diamonds reflecting the different colours from many lights. There were gaily wrapped parcels scattered everywhere and at long benches there were children packing and wrapping as fast as they could.

'What'ur these kids doin' 'ere,' said Harry.

'Ish mish mash,' said Father Christmas, 'and

they're preparing presents for all the good children around the world.'

Harry rubbed his eyes in case he was dreaming, but when he opened them, he found he was still there and he said in disbelief, 'Ooh, that's a lot a parcels. How are we gonna do it in time?'

'Ish mish mash,' repeated Father Christmas. 'We always do it. Here's your name tag. Now be a good boy, go to the book department and wrap some books. You can wrap books can't you?'

'Ooh aye,' Harry nodded eagerly, 'I'm't best in't class.'

'Good, run along.'

Harry jumped down from the sleigh, ran across to a gi-normous mound of books of every shape and size, and started work. There was a thick wad of wrapping paper in front of him, a huge roll of sellotape at the side and his favourite blue plastic scissors and ruler from his school bag.

'How'd they get 'ere,' he mused.

Alongside him there was a little girl sticking labels and rosettes on finished parcels and with a glance at her name label and hoping he might make friends he said politely.

'What'ar ya doin' here, Mary?'

'Boys are stupid, don't you know?'

Harry shook his head in dismay and began to

work. He beavered away for ever such a long time but the pile of books became bigger, the roll of sellotape no smaller and the wad of wrapping paper stayed the same thickness.

He worked faster and faster until his little fingers were hurting from creasing, wrapping and cutting. He fought to keep his eyes open, his head was drooping until he couldn't stay awake any longer. He flopped forward fast asleep onto the table in front of him with the words, 'ISH MISH MASH... ISH MISH MASH,' echoing in his head.

—

Urgent shaking woke him up and he forced his weary eyes open and he saw his Grand-dad wearing a Father Christmas bobble hat standing over him.

'Go'way, I'm tired,' he moaned.

'Ish mish mash.'

Harry groaned, 'What's that?'

The faraway voice of his Mother called out as she came into the room, 'Grand-dad! Put your teeth in. Come on Harry, get up – IT'S CHRISTMAS!'

***

Squirrel Olympics

Jonty and Lilibet were idly passing the time on the Farmhouse window ledge watching the Olympic Acrobatic Championships on Farmer Brown's television.

Jonty, a laid back squirrel, was leaning nonchalantly, arms behind his head with his tail wrapped around him, while Lilibet was sitting on her haunches gnawing on a peanut.

'Oh, she's nice Jonty, the girl from Thailand, but she is tall.'

'What's her name?'

'Long Wan, and she's doing a ball routine.'

'Probably from Pattaya.'

'What makes you say that?'

'I heard young Billy Brown tell his mates that a girl from Pattaya did a great routine with his. Oh dear,' sighed Lilibet, 'she's dropped one. She won't go far.'

'That girl in Pattaya did.'

'Did what?'

'Went all the way.'

'I'm sure I don't know what you mean? Oh look, it's Bronwen from Wales. Oh dear!'

'What's the matter, now?'

'She's got her hand up. I think she wants to go for a leek.'

'That's no good, she'll lose points.'

'They've let her go, Jonty. My Wey from South Korea has taken her place.'

'I expect she'll be doing her own thing.'

'Look Jonty, she's doing a ribbon routine.'

'That girl from Pattaya did that.'

'Did what?'

'Things with ribbons. Billy Brown said she could do tricks for Thailand.'

'Oh dear, Jonty, she's got herself all tied up.'

Jonty scratched himself and observed dryly, 'She should be doing it to someone else.'

'Oh, what a shame, she's retired. It's the Bar now and it's Wan Tun from China. She looks a bit overweight. Be a dear, Jonty and fetch me another peanut.'

'Your wish is my command, oh furry one.'

He stretched and pushed himself upright, flicked his tail and with two bounds leapt across to a drainpipe and hanging on by his claws slid down to the floor.

A quick glance right and left before he ran along the path at the side of the house, staying close to the wall until he came to the back lawn. Pulling himself up to his full height he took a deep breath and ran as fast as he could. The security lamps clicked on and with five strides he went into his routine. A handstand followed by two somersaults and another somersault, a pike with a twist before spotting instantly when he landed.

'Da-Daa!' He took three bows to his imaginary audience before running up the pole to the clothes line stretched across the garden. Showing off his trapeze skills he swung alternately from his front feet to his back feet until he reached the bird-feeder and finished with a flourish by doing two loops hanging on his tail.

Balanced precariously on the line he waved to his audience before lowering himself by his tail until his front feet were level with the bottom of the feeder.

He hung on upside down while fishing a peanut out with one claw. He let the first one fall to the ground and the second one he held in his teeth before pulling himself back up to the line. With a contemptuous flick of his tail he went paw over paw upside down along the line and slid down the pole, ran to the middle, curled his tail around the fallen nut and scampered back to the drainpipe doing two forward rolls for an encore.

He scrambled up the drainpipe and presented his prize to Lilibet.

'Thank you, Jonty, what took you so long.'

He stared at her perplexed and scratched his head in dismay before scooping up a nut and settling back in his corner. The events had changed and Wun Hi of Hong Kong was doing his routine on the men's rings.

Jonty watched disdainfully at the human attempt to copy nature, before saying, 'What happened to Wan Tun, Lilibet?'

'The bar broke, Jonty, too heavy.'

Mrs. Brown walked over to the window and 'swish, swish' the curtains closed.

Lilibet sighed, 'We'd better go home.'

With a flick of their tails and a moments limbering up, they ran to the edge and with legs spread and tails horizontal – GERONIMOoooo – they para-glided to the ground as a fitting end to another Squirrel Olympic display.

***

'Meet the Family'

or

Maybe not

Three words I never use, not since I was a teenager

anyway. 'Meet the family.'

'Why, you may ask?'

I was seventeen when I met this half Japanese girl at high school. She was a real humdinger. Long straight black hair, almond eyes and a honey complexion. Just goddam beautiful in fact. She took me to meet her folks, and just naturally I said, 'You gotta come over and meet ma folks.'

Mistake, a huge mistake.

Take my Dad. He was the local Stationmaster for the Railroad. When I was about twelve Mom said he was going away to do a Master station-guards course. I remember when I was fourteen and exploring my body that, 'My Dad had to go away to learn, this!'

I had a good laugh later when I became familiar

with four syllable words.

'I digress.'

He was a conscientious man and would not touch the demon drink when he was working, but from Friday night until Sunday he would hang one on. He would say to me, 'It's not the beer, son, it's the chasers after.'

I thought to myself, 'If he stopped running they wouldn't chase him.'

Then there's Mom. She was a good mother. We were always clean, the house was spotless and there was always food on the table. Some of it was questionable but it was food. After tea she would drink an awful lot of her 'White wine'. Her argument was that if it was made from berries it had to be wine. I learned later that they were Juniper berries and Gordon's was not a recognised winemaker.

My eldest half brother was Mark. He was Mom's son from her first marriage. He was ugly. His face had more holes and scars than a moonscape and he had a bulbous bright red nose which was also pitted with acne marks. He grew a beard of sorts to try and disguise his problem and he let his hair grow long and dank. Like a Bob Marley bad hair day. Dad said it must have been incest.

He was nice to Mom like that.

Mark made up for it with brains and runs his own

Electronics business. He had a live in girl friend. She was plain, but nice. Mom said she was blind as well.

Now my half-sister Mary is something else. She is Dad's daughter from his first marriage. Like Dolly Parton without the class. She worked nights and came home in a different car every morning. Mom said, 'She must take after her Mother.'

Her one redeeming feature were her fantastic legs and a nice butt. That's something else Mom said, 'Mary's legs ain't never going to be friends as they don't come together often enough.'

Then there's Ellie-May my real sister. She had to drop out of High School on account of her six pound seven ounce problem. Not that she is promiscuous like Mary, 'Oh, no.' She was intelligent and always had good grades but they started sex education in the schools and she flunked the practical.

That leaves me. Like I said, I took my girlfriend to see them and boy o' boy did they frighten her off. I was so embarrassed that I swore I would never take anyone there again.

I got a scholarship to a good University and I joined the flying club there. I graduated with honours in both Math' s and Science and went on to join the US Air Force.

'Your Top-gun material,' they said.

I said, 'No I am not.' I didn't want anything to do

with guns because they shoot back at you, so I flew B52's. After I left the USAAF it was a natural progression from there to flying Lockheed Tri-stars for American Airlines and I was lucky enough to meet this nice flight attendant who worked for British Airways. I followed her to London and transferred to BA. I fly 747's now.

She had to teach me to speak proper English after I frightened the Air-traffic control at Heathrow.

You cannot say, 'Hey, you all down there, I'm a comin' in on Runway two-seven-right, is that okay. What I meant to say was two-seven-left. I lost a months pay for that one.

I now live in Rickmansworth, Hertfordshire, England, and I am a father with a three month old baby girl. She swigs an eight ounce bottle with an enlarged hole in the teat without pausing for breath.

I think she takes after her Grandma but she will never know. Like I told my wife, *'I'm an orphan.'*

***

1883: One Saturday night in Edinburgh

Beware! Naughty!

Ellie demurred long and hard over her choice of dress for dinner that evening and talking to her reflection in the mirror she said, 'I think we will tease our young Lothario tonight.'

Eventually she chose a deep red gown trimmed with black. It had a close fitting bodice, but in keeping with fashion it had the larger bustle that sat high on the hips. The off the shoulder décolletage was low enough to show her birthmark.

She enlisted the help of the room maid to fasten up her hair and decorate it with a black velvet bow before lacing her corset and fastening the innumerable tiny buttons down the back of her dress. A black velvet choker with a diamond clasp added extra allure to her translucent skin.

Mathew called for her at seven forty-five and he stood speechless as he admired the ageless woman before him who carried herself with dignity and elegance.

'You're beautiful,' he said, 'I feel proud and honoured to be your escort tonight.'

'Thank you, young man,' she said with a twinkle in her eye, I shall recompense you later for those kind remarks.'

She picked up her ivory fan. 'Shall we go down?'

He escorted her down the wide stairs her customary shyness evaporating with the presence of her younger companion.

Standing close and exchanging small talk they lingered over a glass of wine with the other guests before they entered the restaurant its decor and subdued lighting designed to give an oyster pink glow.

Dinner was a pleasant interlude with four courses complemented by excellent wines and Mathew took every opportunity to touch her. He reached over the table and held her hand while his knee gently massaged hers. Mesmerized, helpless as a rabbit hypnotised by a stoat, his eyes never left her face the reason for their being together in Edinburgh forgotten.

'Mathew, dearest, do stop looking at me like a lovesick calf. I think people may have noticed and you should remember that we're here on business.'

He jerked upright in his seat searching for words. 'Oh, ah, yes. Your spell had completely erased that from my mind. Ellie Chalmers, unlike medicine, I think that you're not good for me. Oh, that I had met you sooner.'

'Mathew, you are nearly twenty years my junior so nothing would have become of your meeting me then. I was happily married anyway.'

'I know, but a man can dream.'

'Possibly. Let us go through to the lounge these dining chairs were not designed for long conversations.'

'By all means.'

He came around the table to hold her chair and as she turned to move away he leaned forward and whispered, 'I want to make love to you.'

'Behave yourself, Casanova, people are watching.'

'I care not. I am drunk with your very presence.'

'Then you will have to be patient. I would like another glass of wine before bedtime.'

So determined was she to make this young gigolo wait that she took the small talk to its outer limits and made every sip of wine deliberate.

'You should linger over a good wine,' she said provocatively, 'the pleasure lasts that little bit longer.'

Every second was adding to his ardour for this woman in front of him and he tried to suppress his feelings worried that further delay would see an early climax to his passion.

At last, she relieved him of his torment. 'I think it is late enough Mathew. Shall we retire.'

Outside her room, they paused. 'Mathew dearest, I need someone to undo me. Could you oblige?'

Overcome with desire for this woman the direct invitation into her boudoir caught him off guard.

'Aaah, hem, err, yes,' he stuttered.

Taking his hand she led him into the room and stopped in front of the long winged dressing table mirror where she could watch him from all angles.

She stood on tip-toes and nibbled his ear before whispering. 'Undress me.'

 He stood behind her and with shaking fingers tentatively undid the top button, then the next and the next, becoming bolder with each one. He paused, leaned forward and kissed the perfect skin between her shoulder blades and allowed his tongue to brush against the lobes of her backbone. He

felt her shiver as the sensation travelled down her spine.

She pulled on each sleeve in turn and let her dress fall to the floor. Turning quickly, she grabbed his jacket and almost tore it from his shoulders and then frantically pulled off his bow tie and waistcoat.

The pile of clothes grew as the mutual undressing continued. When she stood naked before him wearing only her choker he dropped to his knees and kissed her in that most feminine place. His tongue flicked and massaged the tiny lobe that led to heaven while his hands caressed, searched and fondled.

She sighed and writhed, her breath coming in short gasps. She pushed her hips forward to meet him and pulled his head into her as the tension mounted. Throwing her head back she dug her fingers into his shoulders and moaned. He held her at the peak of her climax, picked her up and carried her to the bed.

Their first coupling was wild, his love making that of a Stag in heat, not the slow ministrations of an older man but the rampant urgings of a young bull intent on propagating his harem. Twice, their ardour was uninhibited before the exhaustion of their lust made them rest.

Later, as they lay curled together like forks in a cutlery box she felt him rising again and she took control by climbing above him. Her lovemaking was slow and deliberate. She held him at his peak and showed him where to touch her so that their eruption was simultaneous and intense.

Passion spent, they slept, entwined in a passionate Gordian knot.

***

LOST & FOUND

Promoted to Sergeant I was sent on attachment to the American Green Berets. Together we went on a 'Hearts and Minds' mission in the Northwest of Laos in an area called the 'Golden Triangle' the centre of the poppy growing industry. It was an attempt to keep the people of the area out of the hands of the commies who were known as the 'Pathet Lao.

The tribes in the area were generally well disposed towards us as the Yanks through the auspices of the CIA paid them the market price for the heroin they produced from the poppies but there was a fly in the ointment. Someone tipped off the bad guys about our movements.

We were two days out from base camp when our

squad of four, three Yanks and myself, were jumped. Two died instantly but Aaron and I escaped after a brief skirmish. The jungle is a friend as well as an enemy and we walked all night and through the next day.

Our complete stock was his backpack with its depleted rations, my Browning 9mm automatic pistol, his M16 carbine and half a clip, my favourite eight inch stiletto and one bayonet cum combat knife. Our compass and maps were lost in the fire-fight and if that wasn't enough he had a serious thigh wound and I had a wound along my ribs which hurt like crazy every time I took a breath.

It was dawn and we were ten yards off the track in primary jungle. The crickets and cicadas are kicking up one helluva din, which is good, and I'm wet through from the water dripping off every leaf.

I'd had a sleepless night keeping watch as there had been movement in the bush during the night and Aaron was moaning in his ruptured sleep. I had to keep him quiet as well as being ready for any eventuality. I think it may have been a tiger but thank goodness we were not on the menu.

I was not a happy bunny but luckily our matches were still dry. That was a blessing as trying to operate the American issue emergency lighter is like trying to light a piece of string in a shower. Anyway, I was able to light the little camp stove. Aaron had not thrown away the rice in his ration pack as we Brits do as a matter of course because it uses too much water so breakfast was half a mug of rice plus a mug of rice water to warm us up.

I used some of our water ration to clean Aaron's wound which didn't look too good and we lay hidden until ten o'clock waiting for the clouds to clear so that we could get a watch sight of the Sun. It's not very accurate but it gives you a rough guide to North and South and by that I was able to steer in what I hoped was a course towards the Mekong River. If we could get to the river plain I could leave him and hopefully cross the river and get help.

We packed our belongings and I went out to the track for a recce. I was relieved to see that any trace of us had been obliterated by the overnight rain.

I tightened Aaron's tourniquet and we set off with his arm around my neck and he used his rifle as a walking stick. I don't know who groaned the loudest, me with the ribs, or him with his leg. Him I guess, and he'd also lost a lot of blood.

I cursed the wet ground as we were leaving tracks a blind man could follow, but luck was on our side. The Pathet Lao had lost our spoor and we stayed safe. The sun came out and with steam rising off our wet clothes we did a three-legged walk towards safety.

An hour later Aaron became too weak and his trouser leg was once more soaked with blood. We stopped to ease the tourniquet and I left him just off the track while I went ahead.

Five minutes later I heard a voice. Positive it was American I pressed on but with a little more caution when the jungle suddenly stopped and I stepped out into a complex of paddy fields in the middle of which was an American helicopter and in the distance the river glistened in the bright sunlight.

My dead reckoning had been good.

'Hey, Mack, get your ass out here,' the pilot was complaining over his radio. 'And bring some frigging hydraulic oil with you.' He went on to give his coordinates before he became aware of me.

'Jeez, what the hell.' In true Mickey Rooney style, not unlike the chopper pilot in the film 'Bridges of Toko-Ri', he ran towards me. 'Hey, what gives, pal? You look like shit.'

I explained the situation and he radioed for a medic and a stretcher as well as his oil.

The pilot was Hank, a New Yorker who chewed incessantly on a cheroot. While we waited for the back-up he came with me to pick up Aaron who was close to dying by this time. His pulse was barely noticeable. Between us we managed to get him back to the helicopter affectionately called a Huey and we waited for the Medi-vac chopper bringing, amongst other things, Hank's much needed hydraulic oil.

When it arrived the medics soon had Aaron on drips and he was loaded into the relief Huey. I stayed with Hank to give him cover while he topped up his oil. He'd repaired the leak apparently before I came across him.

Job done, he cranked up the motor which whined into life at the same time I spotted uniformed figures running towards us.

'Hank,' I yelled, as I scrambled into the left hand seat. 'Get the hell out of here, we've got company,'

'Are ya sure they ain't peasants, buddy?'

'Damned sure.' I pointed in their direction. 'That's not rice paddles their carryin' and they're making poppin' noises in our direction.'

'Jeezuz! Go tell em, wait.'

He jiggled the control levers a couple of times to bleed the system, slid the throttle into the flight idle position and pulled hard upwards on the collective.

The engine screamed and the Huey lifted off. We did a swift torque turn to the left and made a hurried exit. As we did so there was a solid clunk from the engine compartment. A bullet had found its mark.

Nothing appeared amiss and we skimmed at head height over the paddy fields and when we reached the river Hank took us up to two hundred feet and set a course for Ubon in Thailand following the Mekong.

'Shit,' he cursed.

'What's up,' I asked, trying to appear calm.

Hank bit down harder on his cheroot and mumbled through closed lips. 'The collective was heavy when I took her up.'

He eased the cyclical joy stick to the right to correct our course and cursed again.

'Jeezuz man, we're in trouble.'

Now I felt really nervous. As a child I'd had this morbid fear of amusement parks the big dipper in particular and the thought of being suspended beneath a couple of six inch carbon fibre and titanium paddles didn't appeal to me.

I tried to appear calm but my voice went up to a youthful treble. 'Why's that?'

'We're losing hydraulic pressure. That damned bullet must have nicked a pipe.'

The nose dipped sickeningly and we swooped earthwards. My stomach came up to meet my mouth but, 'Oh joy,' I'd had nothing to eat for ages. I then remembered my dangling lap strap and fastened it quickly.

Hank tried the collective and nothing happened. Using all his strength he pulled harder but the sensitivity provided by the hydraulics had gone and the Huey reacted violently. The nose came up sharply in a steep roller coaster climb and our forward speed fell away.

A lesser pilot would have been in trouble but Hank was up to it. He flipped a switch and shut down the hydraulic servo's to all systems which made the chopper just flyable but it would mean considerable physical effort on his part.

Somehow he regained control and he depressed the radio switch on the top of the cyclical to call in. A stream of expletives filled the cabin in a manner that only a man from the Bronx can do.

'They shot up the radio. We're ain't gonna make it, pal,' he yelled.'

I looked at the map and searched around for landmarks. A small island gave me a fix and with a sigh of relief I realised that we were only twelve miles from safety.

'Hank, go right, ninety degrees. We Brits have a camp at Leong Nok Tha. They've built an airfield there and it's my Squadron base. Can you hold her for another few minutes?'

'I'm sure as hell gonna try.'

He kicked down on the right pedal and eased down on the collective lever. With beads of sweat trickling through the dust on his face he executed a tight torque turn before we went into a shallow dive to gain speed on a westerly course.

Somehow he found time to take his right hand off the cyclical column, remove his cap and wipe his forehead with the back of his hand before he pushed the soggy cheroot to the other side of his mouth.

A few minutes later the base came into view and Hank decided we would do an emergency auto-rotational landing into the scrub at the side of the runway.

We circled a couple of times to warn people on the ground while easing down to a safer height for the manoeuvre. With immense effort Hank pulled back on the collective to bring the nose up and stop our forward motion at the same time easing back on the cyclical to put us into the hover.

At this point I found religion.

I watched Hank with admiration as he coolly went through the emergency drill. Once in the hover he closed the throttle, clipped it into manual override and as the revs died down we began to descend kept in the air only by the momentum of the blades.

With a touch of right pedal to stop yaw we came earthward. Six foot from the ground Hank pulled the collective to the maximum lift position using the last bit of available thrust in the spinning rotors to cushion the landing.

All would have been well but for the overgrown monsoon drain at the side of the runway. The left skid dipped into it and the Huey tilted and rolled onto its side. The rotor blades shattered into myriads of pieces and the tail boom crumbled on impact.

Hank, who hadn't fastened his lap strap, tumbled passed me head first into the door pillar and I screamed as my already injured ribs received more punishment. I fell sideways in my seat and my head came into contact with the side of the cabin and all went quiet.

An hour later I woke up staring at the unfamiliar corrugated iron roof of the Station Medical Centre wondering where the hell I was when the unsympathetic voice of Major Gough, my C.O. penetrated my brain.

'You've been living it up with the Yanks too long, Sgt Hunter. A couple of weeks R&R and then you can become a real soldier once more.'

Hank got a lift to Ubon on the back of a low-loader with his broken Huey and I will always be in his debt.

As for my sore ribs. A bullet had smashed the rib and it was pressing into my lung. Aaron survived and he is now a Rabbi in New York. He gave the American Military some cock and bull story and they gave me a Purple Heart, the Medal of Honour and a pension.

***

The life story of George Hunter, soldier and special agent, can be read in my book 'REBOUND which is available on Kindle or Amazon

𝕿𝖍𝖊 𝕰𝖓𝖉

© 2012

𝔄𝔲𝔱𝔥𝔬𝔯 ℌ𝔞𝔤𝔢

About me

My name is JB. Woods and I am a retired soldier and fibre optics industrial operative who has turned his hand to writing after researching my wife's family history which I inspired my first novel. I then joined the 'Paphos Writers Group' and had many short stories published in a monthly magazine and as a result of lessons learnt I edited and ghost wrote other peoples work.

My other exploits into the literary world include **'Stolen Birthright'** a historical novel based on fact. The **Hunter** trilogy - **'REBOUND, Below the Belt and Upstart** fictional adventures of secret agent and soldier George Hunter, and **Henrietta – Tales from the Farmyard,** and most recently: **Tricia - A gardener's daughter.** A historical 19th Century story in the life of a young girl who was left to fend for herself at age of fourteen.

'A Cry of the Heart'— a ghost-written biography and account of the traumatic life story of a young woman from Zimbabwe.

A comedy bonus on the next page.

The Wake

A Yorkshire dialect is good here...

Barnsley about 1970. A living room somewhere in town and Dad is lying in state in the middle of the room. His daughter and her best friend pass the time...

'What were ya Dad's last words, Edie?'

'That were funny, Else, 'Eeh wanted toast.'

'Toast, Edie, how'd yer mean, toast?'

'It were like this, Else. I tek his mornin mug a tea an he sez—'Can I have some toast?'

'Yes, Edie.'

'So I as to go t' corner shop for a cut loaf an I met that Jack Bolsover.

'Who's he, Edie?'

'You know, Him as works on't production line. Is wife's just ad er fifth an her sister's doin well. She's just bought a posh car.'

'Er sister, Edie?'

'Yes, er that works up Love Street.'

'What does she do there, Edie?'

'She's a magician or som'at.'

'Does she play cards then, Edie?'

'I don't know, Else. Our Tom says she does tricks for customers.'

'Oh!'

'What was we talkin' about, Else?'

'Yer Dad, Edie.'

'Ah yes. Anyways, I come home and ad a cup of stewed tea while I pick me losers.'

'Don't yer mean winners, Edie?'

'No Else, I don't ave winners, only losers. Anyway I hears Dad callin' so I goes tot' bottom of stairs an he looked a proper sight wi' is skinny legs under his nightshirt an no teeth.'

'What 'appened then, Edie?'

'I sez, 'Wha' d ya want, Dad?' He let go't banister, shook his fist and shouted, 'Where's me bloody toast,' an he fell down't stairs. He didn't touch till he hit the bottom step.'

'Ooh, nasty, Edie.'

'Aye, Doctor said it were a step too far.'

'So what did ya' Dad do durin't war, Edie?'

'I don't rightly know, Elsie. It were some'at secret.'

'Were he an officer or anything?'

'No, Elsie. Eeh were an NCO. Eeh got a certstif, certisic. You know, a piece of paper off that Field Marshal Montgomery.'

'I got one of them once, Edie, from school. Can a see your Dad's?'

'Ya'll 'ave to ask our Brian. Eeh as a picture of him getting it.'

'What did ya mean, gett'in it. Were he killed then?'

'No, ya daft hay'peth. Getting his bit of paper off Montgomery.'

'Oh, that. I like the box they put im in, Edie. Is it mahogany?'

'You are thick sometimes, Elsie. It's wood. They as to burn im.'

'Oh, right. An what did eeh do after, Edie?'

'After what?'

'The war, Edie, we was talkin' about the war.'

'Oh, right. Eeh went into service an Mam went as cook in't same ouse.'

'Did she ave a cerstificate?'

'Aah don't know, Else, but she were a good cook.'

'Yer right there, Edie. Why're we angin' around?'

'Som'at to do wi' a man an a piece of paper before we can cremate im.'

'Is he comin' then?'

'Who?'

'This Montgomery fella!'

Definitely—THE END

Printed in Great Britain
by Amazon

40456908R00086